TRADITIONAL GREEK HUSBANDS

Notorious Greek tycoons seek brides!

Childhood friends Neo and Zephyr worked
themselves up from the slums of Athens and
made their millions on Wall Street!

They fought hard for their freedom
and their fortune. Now, like brothers,
they rely only on one another.

Together they hold onto their
Greek traditions…and the time has come
for them to claim their brides!

This month Neo's story:
THE SHY BRIDE

Next month meet Zephyr in:
THE GREEK'S PREGNANT LOVER

Lucy Monroe started reading at the age of four. After going through the children's books at home, she was caught by her mother reading adult novels pilfered from the higher shelves on the bookcase... Alas, it was nine years before she got her hands on a Mills & Boon® Romance her older sister had brought home. She loves to create the strong alpha males and independent women that people Mills & Boon books. When she's not immersed in a romance novel (whether reading or writing it), she enjoys travel with her family, having tea with the neighbours, gardening, and visits from her numerous nieces and nephews.

Lucy loves to hear from her readers: e-mail LucyMonroe@LucyMonroe.com, or visit www.LucyMonroe.com

THE SHY BRIDE

BY
LUCY MONROE

First published in Great Britain 2010
Harlequin Mills & Boon Limited,
Eton House, 18-24 Paradise Road, Richmond, Surrey TW9 1SR

© Lucy Monroe 2010

ISBN: 978 0 263 21337 9

Harlequin Mills & Boon policy is to use papers that are natural,
renewable and recyclable products and made from wood grown in
sustainable forests. The logging and manufacturing process conform
to the legal environmental regulations of the country of origin.

Printed and bound in Great Britain
by CPI Antony Rowe, Chippenham, Wiltshire

THE SHY BRIDE

For Robin Hart, a wonderful friend and hypnotherapist,
who has helped me tremendously
through a very difficult time.
Thank you!

PROLOGUE

THE port of Seattle didn't look so different from some of the hundreds of other ports Neo Stamos had been in since joining the crew of the cargo ship *Hera* at the age of fourteen. And yet it was unique from all the others because this is where his life changed. This is where he would walk off the *Hera* and never walk back onto it.

He and his friend Zephyr Nikos had had to lie about their ages to join the *Hera*'s crew six years ago, but that had been a small price to pay in order to leave behind the life they'd known in Greece. Neo and Zephyr had been Athens street thugs that found a common desire—that of making something more of their lives than rising to the top ranks in their gang.

And they were going to do it, twenty-year-old Neo vowed as the sun broke the eastern horizon.

"You ready for the next step?" Zephyr asked in English.

Neo nodded, his gaze set on the port growing closer by the minute. "No more living in the streets."

"We haven't lived in the streets for six years."

"True. Though some would not consider our bunks here on the *Hera* much of an improvement."

"They are."

Neo agreed, though he didn't say so. Zephyr knew and shared his feelings. Anything was better than scavenging to eke out an existence that still required living by someone else's rules. "But what is to come will be even better."

"Yes. It may have taken six years, but we have the money to take the next step in our new lives."

Six years of a hell of a lot of hard work and sacrifice. They had saved every drachma possible of their earnings. For two men who had grown up in an orphanage and then the streets when they ran away, that had been a lot. They knew how to come by clothes, books and other necessities through interesting if not necessarily legal methods. Not unless one considered underage gambling a stumbling block to legality.

When they were not working, or gambling to augment their meager salaries, they had been reading everything they could get their hands on about business and real estate development. Each had become an expert in a different aspect of the field, combining their superior brainpower rather than duplicating effort.

They now had a detailed plan to increase their assets through initially flipping houses and, eventually, full-scale, high-end real estate developments.

"Next it will be business tycoons Zephyr Nikos and Neo Stamos," Zephyr said with conviction.

A slow, extremely rare smile curved Neo's lips. "Before we are thirty."

"Before we are thirty." Zephyr's voice was filled with the same determination Neo felt deep in his gut.

They would succeed.

Failure was not an option.

CHAPTER ONE

"THIS is a joke, right?" Neo Stamos stared at the fancy certificate with the logo of a local charity fund-raiser on it.

His oldest and only real friend, not to mention business partner, Zephyr Nikos had to be kidding. *He had to be*. No way could the certificate be meant for Neo. He had to have gotten it for someone else and was using it to pull Neo's chain before giving it to them.

"No joke. Happy thirty-fifth birthday, *filos mou*." Unlike in the early years of their friendship when they had tried to speak only English to one another to improve their grasp of the language, they now spoke in Greek so they would not forget their native tongue.

"A *friend* would know better than to give me such a gift."

"On the contrary, only a friend would know how appropriate, how needed this little present is."

"Piano lessons?" A year's worth. No damn way. "I don't think so."

Zephyr leaned against the edge of Neo's handcrafted

mahogany desk that had cost more than he had earned his first year of gainful employment. "Oh, I do think so. You lost the bet."

Neo glared, knowing anything he said in repudiation would sound like whining rather than the rational argument it would be. As they had so often reminded each other over the years, a bet was a bet. And he should have known better than to make one with his shark of a friend.

Zephyr's gaze reflected his knowledge of Neo's quandary. "Think of it as a prescription."

"Prescription for what? A way to waste an hour a week? I don't have thirty minutes to waste, much less a full hour." Neo shook his head. There was a reason all of his designer suits were purchased and tailored by an exclusive men's dressing service, and it wasn't because he liked to shout his billionaire status to the world.

It was because Neo Stamos did not have time to shop for himself.

"Unless you know about something I do not…" Like the cancellation of one of their property development projects going on worldwide. "There is no place in my schedule for piano lessons."

Bet or no bet.

"There is definitely something going on you don't know about, Neo. It's called life and it's going on all around you, but you're so busy with our company, it's passing you by."

"Stamos and Nikos Enterprises *is* my life."

Zephyr gave Neo a look of pity, as if the other man hadn't worked just as hard to leave their shared history behind. "The company was supposed to be our way to a new life, not the only thing you lived for. Don't you remember, Neo? We were going to be tycoons by thirty."

"And we made it." They'd made their first million within three years of stepping onto American soil. They'd been multimillionaires a few years later, and held assets in excess of a billion dollars by the time Neo was thirty. Now he and Zephyr were the primary shareholders in a multibillion-dollar company. Stamos & Nikos Enterprises didn't simply bear his name; it consumed his waking and sleeping hours.

And he was just fine with that.

"You wanted to buy a big house, start a family, remember?" Zephyr asked in chiding tone.

"Things change." Some dreams were mere childhood fancy and needed to be left behind. "I like my penthouse."

Zephyr rolled his eyes. "That's not the point, Neo."

"What is the point? *You think I need piano lessons?*"

"As a matter of fact, yes. Even if your GP had not issued you a warning at your latest physical, I would know something has to give in your life. Considering the stress you live under, it doesn't take a doctor to know you are a heart attack waiting to happen."

"I work out six days a week. My meals are planned by a top nutritionist. My housekeeper prepares them to exact specifications and I eat on a schedule more regular than you keep. My body is in top physical condition."

"You sleep less than six hours a night and you do nothing that works as a pressure valve for the stress in your life."

"What do you consider my workouts?"

"Another outlet for your highly competitive nature. You are always pushing yourself to do more."

Zephyr should know. He was right there competing with Neo. So, the other man had started leaving the office closer to six than eight a couple of years ago. And maybe he'd taken up a hobby unrelated to real estate development or investments, but that didn't mean his life was better than Neo's. It was just a little different.

"There is nothing wrong with striving to achieve."

"That is true." Zephyr frowned. "When you have some measure of balance to your life. You, my friend, do not have a life."

"I have a life."

"You have more drive than any man I have ever met, but you do not balance it with the things that give life meaning."

As if Zephyr had any room to talk.

"You think piano lessons will give my life meaning?" Maybe Zephyr was the one who needed a break. He was losing his grip on reality.

"No. I think they will give you a place to be Neo Stamos for one hour a week, not the Greek tycoon who could buy and sell most companies many times over, not to mention people."

"I do not buy and sell people."

"No, we buy property, develop it and sell it. And we are damn good at making a profit at it. Your insistence on diversifying our investments early on paid off, too, but when will it be enough?"

"I am satisfied with my life."

"But you are never satisfied with your success."

"And you are any different?"

Zephyr shrugged, his own tailored Italian suit jacket moving over his shoulders flawlessly. "We are talking about you." He crossed his arms and stared Neo down. "When was the last time you made love to a woman, Neo?"

"We're past the age of scoring and sharing, Zee."

Zephyr cracked a smile. "I don't want to hear about your

conquests. And even if I did, you couldn't tell me about this one because you've never done it."

"What the hell? I have sex as often as I want it."

"Sex, yes. But you have never made love."

"What difference does it make?"

"You are afraid of intimacy."

"How the blue bloody hell did we get from piano lessons to psychobabble? And when did you start spouting that garbage at all?"

Zephyr had the nerve to look offended. "I am simply pointing out that your life is too narrow in its scope. You need to broaden your horizons."

"Now you sound like a travel commercial." And a damn hypocritical one at that.

"I sound like a friend who doesn't want you to die from a stress-related illness before your fortieth birthday, Neo."

"Where is all this coming from?"

"Your GP didn't just warn you at your physical? Gregor took me aside last month during our golf game and warned me that you are going to work yourself into an early grave."

"I'll have his license."

"No, you won't. He's our friend."

"He's your friend. He's my doctor."

"That's what I'm talking about, Neo. You've got no balance in your life. It's all business with you."

"What about you? If relationships are so necessary to a well-rounded life, why aren't you in one?"

"I date, Neo. And before you claim you do, too, let us both acknowledge that taking a woman out for the express purpose of having sex with her, and no intention of seeing her again, is not a date. That is a hookup."

"What century are you living in?"

"Believe me, I'm living in this one. And so are you, my friend. So, stop being an ass and accept my gift."

"Just like that?"

"Would you rather welch on our bet?"

There was no answer for that question Neo wanted to give. "I don't want to take piano lessons."

"You used to."

"What used to? When?"

"When we were boys together on the streets of Athens."

"I had many dreams as a boy that I learned to let go of." Accumulating the kind of wealth currently at his disposal required constant, intense sacrifice and he'd gladly made each and every one.

In the process, he'd made something of himself. Something completely different from the deadbeat father who had taken off before Neo was two and the mother who preferred booze to babysitting.

"Says the man who worked his way off the Athens streets and onto Wall Street."

"I live in Seattle."

Zephyr shrugged. "The stock market is on Wall Street and we lay claim to a significant chunk of it."

Neo could feel himself giving in, if for no other reason than not to disappoint the only person in the world he cared enough about to compromise for. "I will try it for two weeks."

"Six months."

"One month."

"Five."

"Two and that is my final offer."

"I bought a full year's worth, you'll note."

"And if I find benefit, I will use the lot." Though he had absolutely no doubts about that happening.

"Done."

Cassandra Baker smoothed the skirt of her Liz Claiborne A-line dress in navy blue and white oversized checks for the second time in less than a minute. Just because she lived like a hermit in a cave sometimes, that didn't mean she had to dress like one. Or so she told herself when ordering her new spring wardrobe online from her favorite department store.

Wearing stylish clothing, even if said outfits were rarely seen anywhere but her own home, was one of the small things she did to try to make herself feel normal.

It didn't always work. But she tried.

She was supposed to be playing the piano. It relaxed her. Or so everyone insisted, and she even sometimes believed it. Only her slim fingers were motionless on the keyboard of her Fazioli grand piano.

Neo Stamos was due for his lessons in less than five minutes.

When she had offered the year's worth of piano lessons to the charity fund-raising auction, as she did every year, she assumed she would get another student in her craft. A rising star seeking to work with an acknowledged if reclusive master pianist and New Age composer.

Cass unclipped, smoothed and then reclipped her long brown hair at the nape of her neck. Her hands dropped naturally back to the keyboard, but her fingers did not press down and no sound emitted from the beautiful instrument. She had been sure that just like in years past, the auction winner would be someone who shared her love of music. Hadn't doubted that her next student might not share Cass's adoration for the piano.

She'd had no reason to even speculate that a complete musical novice—a tycoon billionaire, no less—would be her student for the next year. It was worse than unbeliev-able; it was a personal nightmare for a woman who found it difficult enough to open her door to strangers.

Trying to circumvent that feeling, she'd spent an inordi-nate amount of time reading articles about him and studying publicity photos as well as the few candid shots of him she'd discovered on the Internet. None of that had helped.

If anything, her worry at the prospect of meeting him had increased. His publicity photos showed a man who looked like he rarely, if ever, listened to any sort of music at all. Why in the world would a man like that want to take piano lessons?

Apparently, he did, though. Because when the bids were well into the tens of thousands, Zephyr Nikos swooped in with an offer of *one hundred thousand dollars*. It boggled her mind—one hundred thousand dollars for one hour a week of Cass's time. Even though the lessons lasted a year, the bid had been beyond extravagant.

The organizer of the fund-raiser had been ecstatic, keeping Cass on the phone long past her usual chat time with people she barely knew. The older woman had waxed poetic about how wonderful it was Mr. Nikos had bought the lessons for his lifelong friend and business partner, Neo Stamos.

And indeed it had been Mr. Stamos's very efficient, and rather aloof, personal assistant who had called Cass to schedule the lesson. Cass had been tolerant because her own practice schedule was flexible and she had almost no social life to speak of.

Regardless, the 10:00 a.m. Tuesday morning classes were hardly a challenge to her schedule. Though Mr. Stamos's PA made it sound like he would be sacrificing something akin to his firstborn child to be there.

Having no idea why a fabulously wealthy, far too good-looking, clearly driven and supremely busy businessman would want the lessons, Cass was even more nervous than usual at the thought of meeting a new student for the first time. In fact, Cass hadn't felt this level of anxiety since the last time she had performed publicly.

She'd been telling herself all morning, she was being ridiculous. It hadn't helped.

The doorbell rang, startling her into immobility, even though she'd been expecting it. Her heart beat a rapid tattoo in her chest, her lungs panting little, short breaths. She turned on the bench, but did not stand to her rather average height of five feet six inches.

She needed to. She needed to answer the door. To meet her new student.

The bell pealed a second time, the impatient summons thankfully breaking her paralysis. She jumped to her feet and hurried to answer it even as worried questions that had been plaguing her since discovering the identity of her new student once again raced through her mind.

Would Neo Stamos himself be standing there, or his PA? Or maybe a bodyguard, or chauffeur? Did billionaires talk to their piano teachers, or keep underlings around to do that for them? Would she be expected to teach with others in the room? If he had them, where would his bodyguards and chauffeur wait during the lesson? Or his PA?

The thought of several people she did not know converging on her home made Cass feel like hyperventilating. She was proud of herself for continuing down the narrow hall to the front door of her modest house.

Maybe he was alone. If he'd driven himself, that opened another host of worries. Would he feel comfortable parking his expensive car in her all too normal neighborhood in west Seattle? Should she offer the use of her empty garage?

The bell rang a third time just as she swung the door open. Mr. Stamos, who looked even more imposing than he did in his publicity photos, did not appear in the least embarrassed to be caught impatiently ringing it again.

"Miss Cassandra Baker?" Green eyes, the rich color of summer leaves, set in a face almost overwhelmingly attractive in person, stared at her expectantly.

She tilted her head back to meet the dark-haired tycoon's gaze. "Yes." Then she forced herself to make the offer she would have to any other student. "You may call me Cass."

"You look like a Cassandra, not a Cass." His voice was deep, thrumming through her like a perfectly struck chord.

"Cass is what my protégés call me." Although referring to this man as a protégé struck her as decidedly off.

As if he found the term as incongruous as she, his perfectly formed lips quirked at one side. Though it could not be called a true smile by any stretch. "I will call you Cassandra."

She stared at him, uncertain how to take his arrogance. He didn't appear to mean anything by it. His expression said he believed it was simply his prerogative to call her by the name he felt suited her, rather than the one she used with the few people she had regular, ongoing communications.

"I believe it will be easier to start the lesson if you let me inside." His voice was tinged with impatience, but he did not frown.

Nevertheless, he made her feel gauche and lacking in manners. "Of course, I…did you want to park your car in the garage?"

He didn't even bother to glance over his Armani-clad shoulder at the sleek Mercedes resting in her driveway before shaking his head, a single economical movement to each side. "That won't be necessary."

"Okay, then. Let's go inside." She turned and led the way to the piano room.

It had been the back parlor when the house was first built in the late nineteenth century. Now it served beautifully to house her Fazioli and practically nothing else. There was a single oversized Queen Anne-style armchair for the use of her rare guests, with a tiny round side table, but no other furniture cluttered the room.

She indicated the wide, smooth piano bench, the same exact finish as the Fazioli. "Have a seat."

He did as she suggested, looking much more relaxed in front of the piano than *she* would have in his high-rise office.

A few inches over six feet, he was tall for the bench, and yet he did not look awkward there.

His body did not have the lithe grace or, conversely, the extra weight around the middle of most male pianists she knew, but was well-honed and very muscular. His hands were strong, with long but squared fingers bearing the wrong calluses for a pianist or a billionaire, if she were to guess it. His suit was more appropriate for a boardroom than her music room, and yet he did not look ill at ease in the least.

Perhaps the sable-haired, superrich Adonis simply did not have the awkward gene like normal people.

"Can I get you anything to drink before we begin?"

"We have already spent several minutes of the hour

allotted for this lesson, perhaps you would find it more efficient to dispense with the pleasantries."

"I do not mind going a few minutes over so you get your full lesson," she said, feeling guilty but equally certain she had nothing to be guilty for.

"I do."

"I see." Strangely enough, his abrupt manner was easing some of her anxiety.

Or was that simply because he had not brought the entourage she had feared? Regardless, she was finding the new situation much less excruciating than she had anticipated. Her gratitude over that fact made her want to be accommodating.

So, no pleasantries then. "Perhaps next week, you should forego ringing the bell and simply come inside," she offered.

His far too compelling green gaze narrowed. "You do not lock your door?" He didn't wait for her to answer before informing her, "I flipped the dead bolt when I closed it."

No doubt a man in his position would find it second nature to double-lock a door behind him. "I'm surprised you don't have bodyguards that have vetted the house."

Really, really surprised.

"I do have security but I do not live a sitcom cop show. You were thoroughly vetted before my PA called to schedule the lessons." He gave her slight frame a cursory perusal. "And you hardly pose a personal threat to me."

"I see." Vague discomfort at the fact she had been investigated settled in her stomach.

"It was not personal."

"Just necessary." As had been her research of him on the Internet.

Although, she suspected the background check done on

her had been far more invasive. No doubt, he knew her history. He was aware of what her manager termed her *idiosyncrasies*. And yet, he did not treat like a freak.

"Exactly." He looked pointedly at his watch. Not a Rolex.

She found that interesting, but didn't comment on it. He'd made it very clear he was there for a piano lesson, not conversation. Again, his brusque approach was unexpectedly comforting.

The remainder of the hour went by surprisingly quickly.

Despite an entirely different sort of tension the tycoon elicited in Cass.

Neo did not understand the sense of anticipation he felt Tuesday morning when he woke and realized his second piano lesson would be today.

Cassandra Baker was exactly as the background check on her had implied she would be. Rather quiet, clearly uncomfortable with strangers and yet something about her charmed him. There were far more important events on his agenda, but his second meeting with the world-renowned pianist who refused to perform publicly was the first one that came to his mind.

Neo could not believe how much he had enjoyed his time with Cassandra Baker.

She was no beauty with her mousy brown hair, light freckles and slight build, and she was not the usual type of woman he found entertaining. More the average "girl next door" and he would readily admit he met few of those in his current lifestyle. And he would not have met her without Zephyr's intervention.

Zee was also the person to introduce Neo to Cassandra's music. His partner had given him her CDs for his birthday and Christmas. Neo started out listening to them when working out on the weight machines, then he would play them sometimes when he was working on the computer. Eventually, it got to where he had Cassandra's music playing pretty much anytime he was home.

He didn't concentrate on who the artist was, just played the music off his MP3 player. He hadn't even recognized her name on the gift certificate for his lessons. Not until the preliminary background report on her came in. That was the first time he realized she composed most of the music he found so pleasing as well.

And he wasn't the only one—Cassandra Baker was a top-selling New Age artist. He would not have expected such a popular musician to be so unassuming. Yet she made no effort to allude to her undeniable talent or fame, further cementing her girl-next-door qualities.

Although undeniably average, her amber eyes were somewhat stunning though, their open and honest expression captivated him and the color was undeniably unique in a way the colored contacts so popular among the artificial beauties he "hooked up" with—Zephyr even had Neo thinking in those terms now—could never be.

Although she wasn't a beauty, Cassandra was intriguing and vulnerable. There was just something about the reclusive pianist he liked. Perhaps it was simply knowing that she made the music that he enjoyed so much.

Whatever the reason, he looked forward to getting to know her better. And when was the last time he had allowed himself the luxury of something so personal not related to sex?

When he arrived at her house, four hours later, he discovered her door on the latch just as she had said it would be. The evidence of her lax security bothered him, but even more worrisome was the sound of music floating down the hall. She couldn't possibly know that he had come inside.

He was frowning when he entered the room she had led him to the week before.

She looked up from the piano, her fingers going still above the keys. "Good morning, Neo."

"Your door was unlocked."

"I told you it would be."

"That is not safe."

"I thought you would appreciate the expediency of getting right to your lesson."

Without waiting for her to offer, he took a seat beside her on the piano bench. "You could not hear me arrive."

"I did not need to. You knew where to come."

"That is not the point."

"Isn't it?" She looked at him as if she truly did not understand his problem.

"No."

"All right. Shall we start where we left off last week?"

Neo was not accustomed to being dismissed, in any form. Yet, rather than get angry, he couldn't help admiring the fact the shy woman had so adroitly shifted focus to the reason he was there.

Which was *not* to lecture her about her habit of leaving the door on the latch, he reminded himself.

He enjoyed Cassandra's soft voice as she guided him through the day's lesson. Her passion for her craft was apparent in every word she spoke and the very way she touched the piano they played. A man would give a great deal to be touched by a lover with such intense dedication.

And his thinking no doubt explained the inexplicable arousal he experienced during something as innocent as piano lessons.

CHAPTER TWO

CASSANDRA covered her mouth as she yawned for the third time in ten minutes. She hadn't slept well the night before each one of Neo's lessons since the first one five weeks ago. In the beginning, it had been her usual anxiety from inviting someone new into her life, even if it was only for an hour a week.

But anxiety had slowly and strangely morphed into anticipation. And she didn't know why. It wasn't as if Neo went out of his way to be friendly. He could not be mistaken for anything but a driven businessman, but she found herself truly enjoying his company. He took his lessons seriously, though it was obvious he did not practice between times.

His manner could best be described as abrupt, often arrogant. Strangely enough, she discovered a peace in his presence she did not experience with anyone else. She tried to analyze it, but couldn't come up with a reason for finding his company so pleasurable.

He'd become less adamant about what she had at first considered the "no pleasantries" rule. He did not complain when she went off on a tangent, discussing her favorite thing—music. He even asked intelligent questions that exhibited both a surprising interest and understanding.

So, she didn't feel too worried bringing up something that had been nagging at her since first meeting him. "You drive a Mercedes."

"Yes." It was clearly an invitation to continue as he played the chords she had just shown him.

"Well, you aren't wearing a Rolex, but you *are* wearing a custom-tailored designer suit."

"You are observant," he said with that little twitch of his lips she'd come to crave in some strange way.

"I suppose."

"But I do not see the point." He gave her a questioning look as his hands stilled on the keys.

"I would have expected you to drive a Ferrari, or something."

"Ah, I see." He smiled.

Really smiled.

And everything inside Cass flipped.

Like *kapow* to her midsection. This was not good. She'd never had a reaction like this to a student, or to anyone for that matter. But, seriously? His smile should come with a warning label. Something like: One glimpse is fatal!

"Few people are open enough to admit when they notice what they consider the inconsistencies of the wealthy man."

"I don't do subterfuge well." She hated social situations to begin with, adding deception to the mix only complicated things to the point of horror for her.

The smile turned into a full-out grin. "That is good to know."

"Is it?" If she'd thought she'd been in danger before, now was absolute Armageddon.

"Yes. Back to your question. It was a question, was it not?" He spoke with a slight Greek accent she found entirely too delicious.

She needed to get out more. Yeah. Right. That was so going to happen. She bit back a sigh. Not. Not going to happen and no matter how lovely she found his accent, it hardly mattered, did it?

It had surprised her at first, but then she'd decided it was to be expected. The information she had found about him online indicated he had left Greece as a young man. However, one article she read said that he spoke Greek with his business partner and had done several property developments in his country of origin over the years.

"Probably a nosy question, but yes," she finally answered.

"I do not mind your kind of nosy. The paparazzi demanding to know the name and measurements for my latest girlfriend is another thing entirely."

Heat suffused her neck and cheeks. "Yes, well, I can guarantee you I won't be asking those sorts of questions."

"No, your curiosity is much more innocent." Which seemed to please him. Odd.

She certainly didn't find her own innocence all that pleasing.

"To answer it, a man does not amass great wealth in a single lifetime by spending his money frivolously. My clothing is necessary to present a certain façade for our investors and buyers. My watch is rated as technically accurate and as sound as a Rolex, but only cost a few hundred rather than several thousand. My car is expensive enough to impress, but not ridiculously so for something that amounts to nothing more than a piece of equipment to get me from Point A to Point B."

"Unlike many men, your car is not one of your toys."

"I stopped playing with toys years before I left the orphanage I never called home."

She'd read that he had lived in an orphanage before leaving Athens. For all that his publicity people allowed the world to know, there was a cloak of mystery around his growing-up years.

Which was something she could understand. While her official biography for publicity purposes revealed that both her parents were dead, it said nothing about her mother's protracted illness. Nor did it mention years spent in a house shrouded in silence and steeped in fear of losing the person both she and her father had loved above all others.

Her father's death as the result of an unexpected, massive heart attack had made the headlines at the time. Mostly because it had heralded the end of rising star Cassandra Baker's public performances. Her withdrawal into seclusion had garnered more press than a good, if sometimes misguided, man's death.

"Some men try to make up for losing their childhood by having a second one."

"I am too busy."

"Yes, you are."

"You did not have a childhood, either." He said it so matter-of-factly.

Like it didn't really matter. And hadn't she decided a long time ago, that it didn't? The past could not be changed.

"Why piano lessons?" she asked Neo, wanting to talk about anything but her dismal formative years.

"I lost a bet."

"To your business partner?" That made more sense than anything she had been able to come up with on her own.

His brows quirked at her description of Zephyr Nikos. "Yes."

"If what you say is true, I wonder how he is rated as being as wealthy as you?"

"Meaning?"

"He spent one hundred thousand dollars on piano lessons you don't want. That sounds very frivolous to me."

"I do want the lessons." Neo looked as if he'd shocked himself with the assertion.

"That's surprising."

"When I was a youth, I wanted to learn piano. There was no chance then. Now, my time is in even shorter supply than money was to my younger self."

"And yet you make the time for these lessons." She could not imagine her own childhood without her piano to take away some of the pain.

"Zephyr does not consider the investment frivolous. He believes I need something besides work to occupy my time."

"For at least one hour a week." Though sixty out of the ten thousand and eighty minutes found in a week didn't sound like much of a relaxing distraction to Cass.

"Precisely."

"Still, he could have gotten you lessons with someone who teaches for a living at a much reduced rate."

"Zephyr and I believe in hiring the best people for the job. You are a master pianist."

"So I have been told." Many, many times since she was discovered as a child musical prodigy at the age of three.

"It is your turn to answer a question for me."

"If you like." And if she could. She braced herself for the question most people asked, and the one for which she did not have an answer anyone had found satisfying thus far.

"Why do you give lessons to the charity auction every year when you are a career composer and pianist, not actually a teacher?"

For a moment, she was so stunned he had not asked what everyone else did—why she had stopped performing publicly—that she was stumped for an answer. Finally, her brain caught up with his curiosity and she said, "Many up-and-coming pianists want to study with me. This is the one chance they have to do so."

"Why present the opportunity at all?"

"Because as much as I prefer a quiet life, one without any new people in it at all can get lonely. And I don't want to be that person. The woman who lives her life as a hermit." Even though in many ways that was exactly what she did.

"Were you disappointed to discover your lessons had been bought by a novice?"

"No, more nervous. Terrified really." She gave him a self-deprecating smile. "I was so dismayed, I begged my manager to get me out of it."

"He did not approach Zephyr, or myself to cancel the lessons."

"No."

Neo's eyes narrowed, but she wasn't sure what was making him look less than pleased. "Why were you so frightened? Even with your condition, you had done this before."

"Not for a successful billionaire."

"I am just like any other man."

It was her turn to frown, unhappy with his false assertion. "For a man who appreciates a lack of deception in others, that lie slid off your tongue rather easily. No way do you believe you are like every other man."

That almost smile touched his features again. "You are more observant than even I gave you credit for being."

"You aren't self-delusional and you aren't like any other man, therefore you could not believe it."

He shrugged. "Few men have the single-minded determination to achieve what Zephyr and I have done."

"And now Zephyr is worried you're too single-minded?"

"I made the mistake of sharing some concerns my doctor voiced on my last physical. Gregor, who is Zephyr's friend as well as my doctor, reiterated those concerns to him."

"The concerns shocked you, didn't they?" she asked, certain she knew the answer and a little surprised at herself for being willing to banter like this.

"How do you know that?"

"You strike me as a man who keeps himself in optimum physical condition as part of maintaining your position at the zenith of personal success. It would astound you that there was some element you had not accounted for."

"I thought you were a pianist, not a psychiatrist."

This, at least, she could explain. "It is easier to watch other people than to interact with them. It naturally follows that someone with my curiosity would try to figure out what makes them tick."

"You are uncannily accurate."

"Thank you for admitting it. I like honesty, too."

"That is something important we have in common."

She shifted beside him on the piano bench, trying to ignore the instant and growing reaction she'd had to his nearness since the first lesson.

"Yes. The other thing is that we both want you to learn piano. Let's get back to it."

Cass had no frame of reference for her response to Neo.

Which was probably why, at twenty-nine she had absolutely no experience in the bedroom. She'd had no time for dating when she was doing concert tours and she'd been doing them since childhood. After stopping public performance, she did not put herself in situations she might meet potential dates. All of which left her in the unenviable situation of being twenty-nine years old and never having been kissed with romantic intent.

And certainly she had never—not once before meeting Neo Stamos—felt this constriction deep in her belly. She'd read about arousal, but never experienced it. Which she knew made her a freak in the eyes of most of the world. But she wasn't just a virgin, she was wholly innocent and unsure how or if she ever wanted to risk changing that state.

When her nipples tightened into almost painful points, she had to bite her lip to keep a gasp from slipping past her lips. And this happened each and every time she sat beside Neo on the piano bench. Sometimes, even without him being there. The memory of their one hour together a week was enough to bring forth her first taste of physical passion.

Alien excitement thrummed through her now, making her thighs quiver and her heart rate increase beyond what even anxiety at meeting a new person produced.

This would never do. She had to get hold of her reactions before she made an absolute fool of herself, but so far telling herself that truth did nothing to diminish this… this…this *ardor* she felt for her student.

She tried to do what she had always done when life got too uncomfortable—concentrate on her music. It didn't always work. Nevertheless, fitting her fingers over the keys, she forced herself to show Neo the newest pattern she wanted him to learn.

"The sound of you playing on this instrument is phenomenal." Neo's deep, approving tones exacerbated each one of the reactions sparking through her.

Cass suppressed a telling shiver. "You should hear it really played."

"One day, perhaps I will."

"Perhaps." Though an invitation to sit in the only chair in the room and listen to her play was one she offered so rarely, even her pushy manager had stopped asking her to make exceptions. "Now you try it."

He stumbled at first, until she laid her fingers over his and led him through it. Which was disastrous for her equilibrium, but pretty efficient in terms of teaching him finger position. By the time his watch alarm went off, he was doing a passable job and she was a quivering mass of nerves hiding beneath her master pianist exterior.

Not so very different from the days when she performed live.

"There are exercises you can do to make your fingers more limber," she told him without looking up. "I suppose suggesting you practice between lessons would be a waste of my breath."

He shrugged. "I am enjoying myself more than I expected to."

"I'm glad." She smiled. "Music is a balm for your soul."

"It can be."

They shared a moment of silent agreement.

He got up from the bench and took a quick glance at his watch with one efficient move of his wrist. "I make no promises about how much practicing I will do, but I will have a piano delivered to my penthouse. My personal assistant will call you for a recommendation."

Neo's personal assistant called, but it wasn't to ask for a purchasing recommendation. It was to cancel Neo's next lesson. He would be out of Seattle the following week.

"Please do not mention this to anyone. Mr. Stamos's whereabouts could cause speculation that might adversely affect his current business negotiations." The woman's tone made it clear that if it had been left up to her, she would have cancelled the meeting without giving an explanation.

Apparently, Neo had felt otherwise. That knowledge made Cass smile, though she promised to be circumspect in perfectly somber tones.

Unfortunately for her, the fact that Neo was out of the city had not made it to the attention of the media, but his weekly visits to her home had.

She woke up Tuesday morning to the sound of car doors slamming and people talking in strident tones outside her home. She rushed to the bedroom that overlooked the street and peeked out through the privacy curtain.

Three media vans and a couple of cars were parked in front of her home. Someone rang the doorbell even as her eyes took in the spectacle before her.

The doorbell continued to ring as she rushed back to her

bedroom to dress. She would just ignore them. She didn't have to answer. She wasn't a public person any longer. The media had no call on her time or her person.

Nevertheless, she skipped her morning shower and pulled her clothes on with haste. Someone banged on the French doors to her bedroom and Cass screamed. Her brain told her it was nothing more than an enterprising reporter who had climbed up to the deck off her bedroom, but familiar panic threatened to immobilize her.

She grabbed the phone off her nightstand and dialed her manager. When she told Bob in short staccato bursts what was going on, he told her to calm down. That this kind of media attention was good for CD sales.

Cass didn't bother to argue. She was trying too hard not to heave from the stress. She hung up and dialed Neo's office, each insistent pound on the glass doors leading to her bedroom making her body flinch.

Her call went to voice mail and she couldn't remember what she said in the message, just that she left one.

She went into the bathroom, shut the door, locked it and prayed for the media to leave.

She was still there, curled up in a ball between the old-fashioned clawfoot tub and the wall, when someone knocked on the bathroom door itself. "Cassandra! Are you in there? Open the door, *pethi mou*. It is Neo."

Neo was out of the city. His personal assistant had said so. She shook her head at the door, another layer of perspiration coming over her already clammy skin.

The knob rattled. "Cassandra, open the door."

The voice sounded like Neo, but she could not accept that he was there. She hated being like this. Didn't want anyone else to know how bad it got, but the rational part of her mind told her to open the door.

The next knock was almost gentle and so was Neo's tone. "Please, little one, open the door."

She forced cramped muscles to work and stood. "I'm…I'm coming," she croaked.

He said something forceful in Greek and then, "Good. Thank you. Open the door."

She reached out and unlocked the door, then pulled it open.

The man standing there did not look like Neo's usual imperturbable self. He wasn't wearing his suit jacket and his expression was nothing less than grim.

She wiped at her face with the back of her hand. "I…they…someone leaked your Tuesday lessons to the media."

"Yes."

"I thought they might come inside."

"It is a good thing they did not."

She nodded, in total agreement.

"You look like you could use a hot shower. I will make you some tea."

"I…yes, that's a good idea." She looked around herself at the bathroom, at Neo, and her gaze skimmed the mirror then went screeching back to it.

She looked like a wreck. She hadn't brushed her hair since waking, her eyes looked haunted, her skin was pale and there were perspiration stains on her shirt. She needed more than a shower. She needed a complete transformation.

But she would have to settle for copious amounts of hot water and the promise of tea.

"Are you all right to be left alone?" Neo asked.

"Yes." Absolutely mortified by her own behavior, she wouldn't have asked him to stay even if it meant losing her piano.

She didn't wonder how he'd gotten into the house until after a twenty-minute shower under very hot water. Mulling the question over, she dried her hair as best she could with a towel. She wasn't going to get an answer until she went downstairs, so she donned fresh clothes and made her way to the kitchen.

Neo was waiting for her in the otherwise empty room. He indicated a mug of still steaming tea on the table. "Drink up."

She sat down and took a sip, almost choking on the sweetness. "How much sugar did you use?"

"Enough."

"For a sugaraholic maybe."

"Sweet tea is good for shock."

"You say that like you know."

"I called my PA, had her look it up."

Cass laughed. She couldn't help it. "I bet she enjoyed that."

Neo shrugged.

"How did you get in the house?" she asked.

"Bob let me in."

"He has a key."

"Apparently."

"I remember him coming," she admitted. She'd refused to answer when Bob knocked on the bathroom door, sure her manager would try to talk her into giving interviews.

"Only one media van remained when I arrived."

"What are you doing here?"

"You left a message on my voice mail."

"I thought you were out of the city."

"I was."

He'd come back. To help her? She had a hard time believing that, but she was glad he was there anyway. She glanced at the clock on the microwave and realized it was already early evening.

She'd spent more than eight hours in her bathroom. No wonder she'd been so cramped when she'd finally stood up. "I feel like an idiot."

"No."

"No?"

"You are no idiot."

She made a sound of disagreement and took another sip of the overly sweet tea.

He sat down across from her. "You have debilitating anxiety related to performing in public."

"Yes, but no one was asking me to perform today."

"Weren't they? Isn't that what the paparazzi do every time they insert themselves into our lives? They demand we perform for them and their audience with a prurient interest in the latest gossip."

"Do you think Bob leaked word of your lessons to the media?" Although she couldn't imagine the furor of this morning caused by piano lessons.

Neo grabbed a tabloid from the counter behind him and placed it in front of her on the table. It had a picture taken through a telephoto lens of Neo entering her house. "They think you're something far more interesting than my piano teacher. They believe you are my latest lover."

She shuddered, not at the thought of being his lover, but at the prospect of being hounded by the media because of the mistaken impression.

"The fact that I kept our relationship secret has given rise to wild speculation and the discovery of your identity only intensified interest."

"I guess it's a good thing you cancelled your lesson for today, or you might have walked right into it all."

He shook his head. "I apologize for what happened. My press manager has released details of the lessons, but I'm afraid at this point there has already been so much conjecture, interest may take some time to wane."

"It's all right. I overreacted."

"Most people would be overwhelmed by a pack of paparazzi on their front step."

"And my back deck."

"What do you mean?"

"Someone climbed the deck and tried to get me to open the French doors to my bedroom."

Fury suffused Neo's features. "That is unacceptable."

"I agree. It was really frightening." But the worst part was that she no longer knew what was normal fear, and what was the result of her abnormal phobia of crowds and public performance.

"That is understandable."

"I don't suppose you want a lesson as long as you are here."

He smiled. "Perhaps, after you have eaten."

Her stomach growled, right then, reminding her that she had not put anything in it since last night. "I'll just have some toast."

But that was unacceptable. He insisted on having one of his bodyguards deliver take-out. When the meal arrived, she surprised herself by being able to eat.

"Your manager wanted to stay and talk to you, but I insisted he leave," Neo said as they were finishing up.

"Thank you. He probably wanted me to do an interview."

"I got that impression." And Neo did not appear impressed by it.

"He told me the publicity would help CD sales."

"When?"

"I called him, before calling your office." She took a sip of the wine that had arrived with the meal. "I'm not sure why I called your office, now that I think about it. I wasn't exactly thinking rationally."

"I am glad you did. Clearly I am the reason for the problem. I should effect the solution."

"I think, Neo Stamos, that you are a good man."

He looked absolutely stunned by her words, but quickly masked his shock. "I take that as a compliment."

"I meant it as one."

They didn't end up having a lesson that evening, but Neo stayed until nine, when the wine and the release of adrenaline caught up with Cass and she began yawning every other minute.

"You need your rest."

"I do." She laughed softly. "I'm exhausted, though I shouldn't be."

"Of course you should. Sleep."

"I will."

She thought he was going to kiss her when she let him out the front door, but he only squeezed her shoulder and told her again to get some rest.

She shook her head at her own foolishness. Why would a man like Neo Stamos want to kiss her? Cass wasn't in his league in any shape or form. And then there were her "issues."

She wasn't housebound. She could buy food on her own without getting overly stressed as long as she went to the local grocer she'd been going to since she was a child. Although she did most of her other shopping online, she could go to familiar department stores, if she really needed to. She had overcome most of her anxiety related to recording at the studio, so long as the technicians and music producer did not change. And her manager didn't bring anyone in to watch her record.

Bob had stopped doing that after the last time she'd simply refused to play and gone home.

But today proved that she wasn't approaching normal, either. Her agoraphobia was mostly limited to performing, but the prospect of having strangers in her home, her sanctuary, always engendered deep anxiety in her. The barrage of media outside her home had brought back debilitating memories.

She had no idea how long she would have remained in her en suite bathroom if Neo had not shown up. Certainly, knowing Bob was there earlier had only increased her stress levels, knowing as she did how he would want to capitalize on the situation.

She really didn't understand why Neo's presence had made such a difference, but she was unutterably grateful it had.

CHAPTER THREE

THE following morning, Cass was working on a piece she planned to cut onto her next CD when the doorbell rang. She ignored it. There had been no media vans outside her home this morning and Neo had released a statement that should set most wagging tongues at rest. But that didn't mean an enterprising reporter would not come back looking for a quote from "the recluse pianist."

Even after learning the truth, there would be some who insisted on believing the billionaire and Cass had some sort of relationship. After all, that made better news copy than the fact he was taking piano lessons.

Besides, it wasn't completely out of the norm for her to get the occasional door-to-door salesman, despite her No Solicitors sign right above the doorbell.

She felt no compunction about ignoring *visitors* who paid no attention to her clearly stated wishes. And she definitely did not want to talk to a reporter, no matter how much her manager Bob, might wish otherwise. She was feeling a lot calmer today than she might have expected, but Neo's company the night before had helped settle her in a way even her father had been unable to do after a performance.

She'd felt safe when he was there and had trusted him to do his best to right the media mess.

The doorbell rang again, but her friends and business acquaintances knew to call first, so she continued to pay it no heed.

Then the phone rang.

She sighed with frustration, but got up. This piece was never going to gel with this kind of interruption. She grabbed the phone and answered it. "Hello?"

"Miss Baker?"

"Yes." What was Neo's PA doing calling her? Oh, right. "You're calling for the piano recommendation."

"Actually, no."

"No?" Disappointment filled her. "Does Mr. Stamos need to cancel his lesson for next week as well?" she asked.

Had he decided to stop them all together? She wouldn't blame him after yesterday.

"No."

"Oh." Maybe she should just wait until the other woman came to the point. Guessing games got annoying when they didn't bear immediate fruit. And she didn't like the answers her own brain was supplying so far.

So, Cass waited in silence for the PA to do just that.

The other woman cleared her throat. "Mr. Stamos asked me to schedule a locksmith to come out and fix the handle on your front door and add an additional lock to a set of French doors on your upper floor. The locksmith is there, but apparently your doorbell is not working properly."

"It's working just fine."

"The locksmith rang it. Twice."

"I do not answer my door when I am not expecting company." Cass did not make any further explanation. She'd learned a long time ago that trying to explain her idiosyncrasies only made matters worse.

Particularly with people like the cold-fish personal assistant employed by Neo Stamos.

"If you do not answer your door, the locksmith cannot fix the door handle problem."

"What problem is that exactly?" She hadn't noticed any trouble with her door handle sticking, though she was willing to entertain the possibility Neo had spotted something she missed when he had been there.

"Mr. Stamos left instructions for it to be replaced by a self-locking model."

"Mr. Stamos left instructions with you about my door?" she asked, stunned. "Without informing me?"

She knew he didn't like her practice of leaving the door on the latch when she was expecting company. It was part of her mental preparation for visitors—reminding herself she needed to be open to other people, at least in some limited capacity.

He complained about it every week, but did he really expect her to replace the handle because of it? Surely he realized she wasn't going to leave the door unlocked right now. Not with the paparazzi entirely too interested in her and Neo's association.

"I really can't speak to whether or not he informed you. I only know my instructions."

"You expect me to allow a perfect stranger into my home to replace my door handle, on your boss's say-so. When I did not request, much less authorize this *upgrade*?"

She used the word for lack of something better, though Cass wasn't convinced it was any such thing.

The personal assistant's silence said that was exactly what she expected.

She'd thought Neo understood. At least a little. Apparently she'd been wrong. "No."

"No? But Mr. Stamos—"

Cass felt no compunction in interrupting the officious woman. "Please call your locksmith and cancel the order. Right now."

"I can't possibly. Mr. Stamos—"

"Does not own this property. And, I, *the owner*," she added, her anxiety creeping through, "have no intention of replacing my perfectly functioning door handle."

"Mr. Stamos will not be happy about this," the PA warned ominously.

"I'm sure Mr. Stamos has many other things of much more importance for him to concern himself with."

"No doubt, but he left instructions."

One thing that could be said for Neo, he engendered loyalty and commitment to follow through from his employees.

"He should have run those instructions by me," Cass said with little sympathy. *She* wasn't one of Neo's employees. And if he had done so, she could have assured him she wouldn't be leaving the door unlocked for the foreseeable future.

"Mr. Stamos is not in the habit of asking the opinions of others."

"Really? I never would have guessed," Cass replied just a tad sarcastically. Then she winced at her own behavior. She knew Neo was just trying to make things better. He'd simply gone about it the wrong way. Because no matter how she might wish otherwise, he did not understand. "Cancel the locksmith."

An unmistakable huff of annoyance sounded over the line. "I will inform the locksmith his services are not required at present. Mr. Stamos will be made aware the delay is at your demand." The frigid tones of the personal assistant should have frozen the phone lines.

"You do that. You can further inform your boss that if my practice session is interrupted by the locksmith, or any of his other employees, he will spend *his* next lesson listening to me prepare my own music rather than teaching him his."

The silence that met her words actually brought half a smile to Cass's face. It was an empty threat, but it had felt good saying it. Would Neo see the humor in it, or would he lack understanding of that, too?

"I shall pass on your message verbatim," the other woman finally said.

"Thank you."

Neo was furious with himself. He should have called Cassandra and warned her about the locksmith, even gotten that annoying manager of hers to be there to supervise the changing of the locks. Instead, he'd left instructions with his PA as he always did and this was the result.

He had to smile at Cassandra's threat however. Getting a private concert from the superbly talented pianist would hardly be a hardship. Regardless, he felt badly. Which was a completely uncommon reaction for him. So was the acknowledgement that he had messed up. Both of which were the reasons he was calling Cassandra on his personal cell phone, in the middle of a corporate conference call with the project team in Hong Kong.

He muted his headset and listened with one ear while dialing Cassandra's number and then listening to the line ring.

"Hello?" she answered on the third ring, sounding downright cranky.

And why he should find that charming rather than annoying he could not have said.

"You sent my locksmith away."

"Actually, your personal assistant sent him away. I did not answer the door."

"Why?"

"I thought he was another reporter."

Neo had to stifle a groan at his own idiocy. He should have expected that. "I meant why did you send him away?"

"Why didn't you ask me if I wanted my door lock changed?"

"It needs to be done. You can't remember to keep your door locked."

"I don't forget; I just choose to leave it unlocked when I know someone is coming."

"That's not much of an improvement."

"I don't plan on leaving it unlocked anytime soon, if that makes you feel any better. I don't want reporters walking in on me unannounced."

"Some would, regardless of trespassing laws."

"Yes, the person who climbed onto my deck certainly wasn't worried about trespassing."

"For all your unwillingness to entertain strangers, you are much too lax when it comes to your personal safety. The locksmith was only a stopgap measure anyway. You need a full spectrum security consult."

"Not going to happen." There was not the slightest uncertainty in her voice.

Neo had gone against tougher negotiators than the
renowned pianist. "Consider it a gift for opening your
home to me."

"Are you saying this is for *your* safety?"

"Would it help you accept it if I did?"

"For an honest man, you're awfully adept at manipula-
tion."

"Thank you."

"I am not letting a stranger into my home."

"I was a stranger when you allowed me inside for my
lesson." But he could see now that he'd made a grave mis-
calculation in sending over an unknown locksmith.

Zee warned Neo that his impatience could cause problems
and this wasn't the first time his friend had been right.

"Not entirely. One, I had prepared myself for taking on
a new student. Two, I did my research, learning all I could
about you before you came. And three, my manager told
me if I didn't do the lessons he would quit."

"You got past being overwhelmed by me—you can deal
with the security consultant."

"No."

"Cassandra, you are not being reasonable."

She laughed, the sound both exasperated and amused.
"*I* am unreasonable?"

"Yes. It will only take thirty minutes, an hour at the most."

"It's not just about the time, but that is a consideration."

"The security expert can work around your schedule."

"I don't want to meet him." She sounded very definite.

"Cassandra, be sensible."

The quality of the silence at the other end of the line

bothered him. "If you are that concerned," she finally said, "we could probably arrange to have your lessons at my recording studio." She was silent again, this time clearly considering her own proposal. "Yes, that would work."

"I do not want my lessons at the studio."

"I do not want to entertain a stranger in my home." The growing agitation in her voice bothered him.

He did not like to think of his shy teaching aficionado getting upset.

"If I were there for the security consult, would you be all right then?" Neo absolutely stunned himself by asking.

From the expression on his PA's face she was similarly flummoxed.

But Cassandra had come out of her self-imposed prison of the bathroom yesterday for him when she had refused for her manager. Neo was used to being relied on by his employees and associates. It shouldn't make him feel special that Cassandra naturally did as others before her, but somehow it did.

"What? You be here? No. You're too busy. That's not necessary." Cassandra took an audible breath. "Look, I'll…I'll ask my manager. He'll come meet with the security consultant. He thinks these lessons are good for my career, though I really didn't understand why until the whole media fiasco yesterday. Bob will do it."

Unfamiliar amusement welled up, along with a highly out-of-character tolerance. He'd broken her brain. He must have broken his own as well because he didn't want Bob to be the one helping her deal with this, even though that had been his own idea not fifteen minutes ago.

"You don't want to be there for the consult at all? As you reminded my personal assistant, it is *your* home."

"Yes, well… Are you sure you don't want to meet in the studio?" she asked, sounding entirely too hopeful for a woman who spent so much of her time in her home.

Ignoring the repeated offer, he brought his schedule up on his phone. He marked two items for his PA to move and said, "I'll be there with the consultant tomorrow morning at ten."

"You don't have to. I said—"

"If your manager was capable of convincing you to implement better security, he already would have done so."

"I didn't have a billionaire student before."

"Nevertheless, the man is clearly incompetent when it comes to assuring your ongoing personal safety."

"I'm sure that you have a big need for personal security, but I'm a moderately successful musician. I don't even tour."

"You are a brilliant musician with a large fan base, despite your unwillingness to do live performances. You should have implemented additional home security long ago."

"I can see your point of view, but it's skewed by your lifestyle." She sounded just a tad desperate, though he couldn't begin to understand why. "You've got to be able to see that."

"I prefer not to waste time in useless argument."

"Good."

"I'll see you tomorrow morning."

She was still spluttering when he disconnected the line.

Cass glared at the phone, and then picked it up and dialed the number that showed up on her caller ID.

He picked up on the first ring. "Further argument will only serve to annoy me."

"How interesting." Neo really must get an unhealthy dose of arrogance with his morning coffee. "It is customary to say goodbye when hanging up. Please remember that in future."

"Duly noted. Goodbye."

"Goodbye."

She distinctly heard a chuckle as he once again ended the call.

Smiling for no reason she could fathom, especially considering what she had just agreed to, Cass went back to practicing her piece. When a certain set of green eyes kept interrupting her flow of thoughts and she found her fingers moving in a Vivaldi concerto segment she found particularly passionate, Cass knew she was in trouble.

True to his word, Neo arrived at exactly 10:00 a.m. the following morning. Her hair in a smooth French twist and wearing a bright pink Jackie-O style dress with matching jacket for courage, Cass was waiting for him in the music room, but she heard the low purr of his Mercedes as he pulled into her driveway.

She couldn't even pretend to play to settle her nerves. Neo was bringing a stranger who was going to make changes to her home. Changes that she would still be getting used to when his year's worth of lessons were over.

He rang the bell, but tried the handle as she had suspected he would. She heard the latch give and then footsteps. The door shut. More footsteps, Neo's distinctive purposeful tread and a quieter walk, though no less confident.

A few seconds later, Neo led a shorter, blond-haired man into her music room.

"Cassandra." The tycoon gave her a chiding look. "You left the door unlocked. You said you wouldn't."

"I only unlocked it a few minutes ago. I knew you would be on time."

Frowning, he shook his head. "What if traffic had prevented our timely arrival?"

"It wouldn't dare."

He didn't ask why she hadn't simply waited to let them in when they arrived and she was grateful. She had needed this one small coping mechanism this morning.

Having the security consultant over was such a simple thing, one that would not bother normal people, but Cass wasn't normal. She'd figured that out long before she understood what her idiosyncrasies would mean in her life.

Taking a firm grip on her irrational sense of dread, she turned to face the blond man. "I'm Cassandra Baker. Welcome to my home."

The security consultant put his hand out, "Cole Geary. It's an honor to meet you, Miss Baker. I'm a huge fan. I've got all your CDs."

She shook the man's hand and gave him her smile for public consumption. "Mr. Geary, it's a pleasure to meet you. I'm glad you like my music. It's the joy of my life."

"You can tell, the way you play, I mean."

Neo cleared his throat, giving them both his look that was probably supposed to mean, "Wasting time here, people."

Cole's expression went from open admiration to professional in a single blink. "Mr. Stamos has expressed some concern over your security here. Would it be all right if we took a look at the premises before I make any preliminary suggestions?"

The proper response would have been, "Of course not." Only she didn't want Cole Geary in her home. No matter how big a fan, or how nice he seemed.

"I don't want bars on my windows," she blurted out rather than answer his request. She lived with enough limitations caused by her own nearly debilitating shyness.

"As I said—"

"It will be all right," Neo said, interrupting his consultant. He laid his hand against the small of Cass's back. "Let's show Cole the rest of the house."

She looked up at him, begging him to understand the emotions roiling inside her, feelings that had both plagued and shamed her since childhood. The one and only therapist she had seen at her father's insistence had done little to help Cass overcome her anxiety. Though the man had helped her learn some necessary coping mechanisms.

He had once explained that her experiences growing up in the house of an invalid, combined with the pressure to perform at a young age, had severely exacerbated what had probably been a simple case of being a more timid personality type. That was his theory anyway.

All she knew was that she currently suffered a mild form of agoraphobia fed by sociophobia, though how mild she often wondered. Especially when she felt so completely out of her depth doing something as simple as meeting a security consultant and showing him her home.

"I should have had Bob meet you," she said so quietly she wasn't sure he would hear her.

"Trust me, Cassandra." Neo focused one-hundred percent of his attention on her, totally ignoring the other man for the moment. "You and I will do this together."

"I'm being ridiculous." She hated putting herself down like that, no matter how true she knew the words to be.

She just got tired of admitting such unpalatable truths about her reactions, particularly when she felt powerless to change them. It was one of the reasons she hesitated making friends. New relationships required fresh acknowledgement of the limitations she and the people in her life had learned to live with.

Neo shook his head decisively. "It is the world you live in. If you will but trust me, you will see there is nothing to worry you."

"My father used to say the same thing." Right before forcing her onto a stage where she had to lose herself in the music or lose her sanity, or so it felt to her.

She could remember the sea of faces that would confront her at each sold-out concert for the child prodigy pianist. And that memory still had the power to send a cold sweat down her spine. For as far back as she could remember, her music had always been a deeply personal thing for Cass. She used it to hide from the reality of her mother's illness and her father's often angry helplessness in the face of it.

How Cass had hated sharing her music with crowds of strangers, too many of whom wanted to meet the young pianist, after what had always been for her a soul-exhausting concert.

Something moved in Neo's green eyes. "You will tell me about that later, but realize I am not your father."

"No." The feelings she experienced in Neo's presence were far from familial. And he was not cajoling her to perform in a packed auditorium. She took a deep breath and let it out. "Okay. We can show him the house."

"Let's do this," Neo said to Cole.

The security consultant simply nodded, without giving Cass any of the strange looks she was used to receiving when her limitations got in the way of normal social interaction.

Gratitude washed over her and she gave him a genuine, if small, smile.

Then, despite the fact the man had gone past the music room and the hall only once before and that was yesterday, Neo led them on a flawless tour of *her* house. It was uncanny. He never once opened a closet door expecting a room, or missed a door that led to the outside. Although her house was small, there were four doors of that nature—the front door, the kitchen door, and French doors in both the master bedroom and dining room. Those in her room led out to a raised deck and the ones in the dining room opened onto the patio below that deck.

"Ideally, we would replace these doors with ones made of reinforced metal and shatterproof glass," Cole said, eyeing the bedroom's French doors with disfavor.

Cass gripped Neo's suit jacket without thought. "Neo," she pleaded. "Is that really necessary?"

"You will spend the day with me when the renovations are being done."

That was not what she had asked, nor should it have made her feel any better. After all, *Neo* was really just a student, not a friend or a protector, but he made her feel safer than she had in years. Maybe ever.

And wasn't that thought just a tad overwhelming. Neo would walk out of her life without a backward glance in less than a year's time. His lessons would be over and he would move on, but Cass did not think he would leave her unchanged.

And maybe that was okay.

It had been too long since she let anyone inside, but even if it led to pain and loss down the road, it might well be worth it.

"I'm sure your personal assistant will love that. She doesn't like me," she said to cover her nearly overwhelming relief at his offer.

Cass could not imagine spending the day trailing after the high-energy billionaire. But for the first time in years, just because she couldn't imagine it, did not mean she refused to try it.

"Miss Park? She is a very efficient personal assistant. I do not pay her to like or dislike people."

"Just because you don't pay for it, doesn't mean you don't get it." Did the man really think people worked that way?

"I have acted somewhat out of character in my dealings with you. No doubt that surprises her."

"Really?" Cass let go of his jacket and smoothed the expensive fabric. "I guess that *doesn't* surprise me. Even I realized you offering to come this morning was not the norm."

"No, but here I am."

"Why is that?" she asked. Was it possible he felt the same almost primal connection she did? And what would she do if he did?

No way would a dynamic man like Neo Stamos tolerate the cramp in his style a relationship with her would cause.

"I believe I am making a new friend for the first time in more years than I care to count."

"Oh." Of course he hadn't felt the same amazing attraction. Neo was surrounded by gorgeous, fully socially functional women. Cass wouldn't even register a blip on his female companionship radar, but friendship wasn't something to dismiss lightly. Not for her anyway. She didn't have so many she could or would want to dismiss his offer. "I think I'm honored."

"As am I, by your trust."

"I do trust you."

"I noticed."

Cole cleared his throat. "I've seen enough to write my preliminary report."

Neo's face twitched just enough to let her know that like her, he'd forgotten the other man was there.

"Good. I'll expect it on my desk by afternoon."

"For the rates you're paying, I can make that happen." Cole smiled as if he didn't mind rich clients throwing money at a problem they expected him to fix.

It was a good attitude to take, she was sure. If you wanted to keep working for said rich clients.

"I'd like to see the report as well," she said.

Cole's smile warmed up a couple of degrees as he turned it on her. "No problem."

"Naturally," Neo said at the same time.

And then like the whirlwind he was, Neo Stamos was gone, his security consultant along with him.

CHAPTER FOUR

CASS read the security report, her heart sinking further with each recommendation.

No way was all of this going to be done in one day, or even two. Despite most of the security upgrades being offered with options that made them as unobtrusive to her current lifestyle as possible, they were far too extensive for a single-day implementation. Looking at the report, she had visions of workmen coming and going, invading each and every room of her sanctuary, for a week at the least.

She appreciated Cole's efforts to keep the changes in the background, she really did. Just as she was grateful he had brought the report personally, instead of sending a messenger as he told her he had done for Neo.

However, no amount of understanding on the part of the security expert could alter the fact that he was recommending several anxiety-producing modifications to her home. Not least of which was a state-of-the-art alarm system that governed every window and door in her house.

Should she accidentally set the alarm off, a hundred-plus decibel noise would assault her ears and those of her neighbors. Not only that, but the system would be hooked into his private security company for twenty-four-hour monitoring. Someone there would have access to duplicate keys to all her outdoor locks. Even though Cole called the system typical in its implementation for residential security, Cass felt like it was all too cloak-and-dagger for words.

Cole had also recommended replacing all of her doors and windows with more secure models. He wanted to install biometric locks as well. She knew biometric referred to locks opened with retinal or fingerprint scanners, which almost sounded intriguing, if a little redolent of science fiction. She might actually like that upgrade.

But by far, the worst elements to the proposal, and the ones given the least explanation, were those recommended for the outside of her home. Cole wanted to cut back the lilac bushes her mother had planted the year Cass's parents had moved into the house. And that was only the beginning of the landscape changes he wanted to make outside.

There was nothing for it. If Neo's privacy and safety were the reasons for the upgrades, Neo would simply have to have his lessons in the studio. Which is what she told him when she called him a few moments later.

"We have already discussed that option and I do not find it acceptable."

"Then we'll have the lessons at your penthouse." Why hadn't she thought of that before? "You're planning to get a piano anyway. It would be beneficial to have your lessons on the instrument you use for practice."

"What is the problem here?" he asked without a sign of impatience, which rather surprised her. "I have looked at

the report and I thought Cole Geary did a fair job of mini-
mizing the impact of the improved safety measures."

She rolled her eyes, though of course he couldn't see.
"For someone like you maybe."

"Someone like me would require an armed guard on the
premises at all times."

"Sucks to be you." The words just slipped out, but she
meant them. With every fiber of her being. She could not
imagine spending her days under constant observation.

A surprised bark of laughter sounded. "I've got to admit
that is the very first time in my adult life that particular
phrase has been directed at me. What is even more astonishing is that I can tell you mean it."

"The life of a high-profile businessman is not for me,"
she said, amusement making the first tiny cracks in the wall
of anxiety that had been building since she had agreed to
have the security consultant come over yesterday.

"It's a good thing you are just my friend, not my business partner." He sounded like he was smiling, if not laughing outright.

"I'm sure Zephyr Nikos is grateful for that as well," she
said dryly.

"I don't know. I can push too hard at times, but then
so can he."

It amazed her how humble the tycoon could sound after
all that he had accomplished in his thirty-five years. She
couldn't afford to get sidetracked by admiration though.
"I, on the other hand, may not be pushy, but I am also not
a pushover."

"I never thought you were. It takes determination to
refuse the lucrative life of a concert performer."

"My manager calls it bullheaded stubbornness."

"Naturally, the more money you make, the more he does."

"That's one way to look at life."

"Are you saying you don't think he does?"

"Honestly? I don't know. When my father died, I clung to Bob because he was someone familiar. I assumed he had my best interests at heart, and mostly, I think he does."

"But he is motivated by a desire for financial success like so many of us."

"Oh, I don't think it's mere money that motivates you. I get the feeling you like being a rich man, but you enjoy being a powerful one even more."

"You think so?"

"I do. You wear the mantle of control with complete comfort."

"This is true, but what makes you say so?" His tone couldn't be mistaken for anything but genuine curiosity, no defensiveness there.

She laughed. She couldn't help herself. And then she laughed some more. When she finally got her mirth under control, she was met by silence at the other end of the phone.

"Are you still there?"

"Yes. Are you finished laughing?"

"Um…I think so."

"It is another first for me."

"What?"

"Being laughed at. Even Zephyr would not dare."

"Oh, come on. You trip and fall and your best friend would not laugh?"

"I would never trip and fall."

"I suppose you never spill sauce on your shirt at a restaurant, either."

"No."

"Hmm…you never mistake someone's identity in an embarrassing and amusing-to-your-friends way?"

"I do not make mistakes."

"You sound like you mean that."

"I also do not say things I do not mean."

Wow, such arrogance.

"Even when you are negotiating a real estate deal?"

"I never bluff."

"Oh." For some reason that was just a little nerve-wracking to know.

"Should I apologize for finding you funny?" she wondered out loud.

"Not necessary, but I would appreciate you sharing the joke."

"You."

"I am the joke?" he asked in an odd voice.

"Um…yes."

"Explain."

"Neo, you have done nothing but boss me around since the moment I met you. Your control issues are hardly a deeply-seated psychological secret."

"I do not have issues with control," he replied with clear affront.

She almost laughed again, but she managed to stop herself with a judicious bite to her lower lip. It hurt, but it was effective. "No, you just insist on being the one who has it."

"I cede control when necessary."

"Which I'm sure isn't often."

"True, but there is nothing wrong with that." His tone was almost defensive this time.

She couldn't quite stifle the grin that caused, but she tried very hard not to let it show in her voice. "If you can handle the stress of so much responsibility, maybe not, but your insistence on changing my home to suit your whim *is* taking it a bit far. If you don't mind my saying so."

"We have discussed this. Concern for your safety is hardly a whim."

"I thought we were implementing these changes for *your* safety."

"Yesterday was disturbing for both of us. And I have bodyguards."

"I see." She'd thought as much, but when he had been so insistent, she'd been unable to comprehend him being that way for her sake rather than his own. "I don't want to change my house *for me*."

She didn't want to change it at all, but particularly if the reason for doing so was some spurious need to increase her personal safety. She had lived her whole life in that house and was doing just fine. Even alone, like she had been since her father's death.

"Consider, if the ruthlessly forward reporter that climbed your back deck had broken one of the glass panes on the French doors to your bedroom. Which he could have done all too easily. He could have gotten inside. Even if his intention was not to harm you, such an action would cause you grave distress."

"There's no reason to believe there will be a repeat of yesterday anytime soon, if ever."

"You are a celebrity. You may be a shy one that does not court the spotlight, but with the increase in sales on each new album, you build a wider and wider fan base. An incident just like yesterday's could indeed happen again, and *soon*."

She shivered, feeling slightly nauseated at the prospect. Still, she had stopped being a public performer years ago.

"Even though I have reasonable success with my music, I'm hardly at risk like a pop star."

"But you are at risk."

"Why are you so insistent?" she asked almost plaintively.

"It is what is best for you. I am used to doing what is best for the people who rely on me."

"I am not one of your employees."

"It does not matter." He sighed, as if exasperated. "I have already arranged for payment if that is what concerns you."

"You know it's not."

"Cassandra—"

"I'll see you next week. Let me know if you wish to meet at the studio or your penthouse."

He said her name again, but she simply said, "Goodbye," at the same time.

She hung the phone up without another word.

Cass wished she was surprised when the doorbell rang the next morning before she'd even had her first cup of coffee, but she wasn't. She was even less surprised to look out the window in the bedroom that overlooked the drive and see Neo's Mercedes parked there.

He was not the type of man to let someone else set terms. Besides, no matter what she thought, he was convinced she needed to upgrade her house's security.

She was less than halfway down the stairs when the doorbell rang. Impatient and quick, Neo didn't linger on the doorstep dithering about whether or not to bother her so early in the morning as she would have done. She didn't even consider trying to ignore the bell, or the man ringing it.

Neo would not be deterred by a mere refusal to answer the door. Besides, as much as she hated confrontation, she did not hide from it when necessary. And it was necessary to make Neo understand she wasn't transforming her home on his whim.

All words along that vein and any others dried up when she swung the door wide to be confronted by the man in person. He was so darn gorgeous in today's business suit, each dark hair perfectly in place, his green gaze locked on her with laserlike intensity.

She went hot all over and stopped breathing. For just a few seconds, but it was enough to remind her how out of control she felt in his presence.

Why did he affect her this way?

It was like the anxiety she felt at being in a crowd of strangers, only not. Because as unsettling as this feeling was, she liked it. She liked him.

Even when he was trying to boss her around.

He'd opened his mouth to speak, but shut it when he saw her. "What are you wearing?" he demanded after several seconds of silence.

Not sure what had him so confused, she looked down at herself. Yes, she *had* remembered to don her robe. The teal blue silk covered her from neck to ankle in more than adequate modesty. Her feet were bare, but she was in her own home, surely that wasn't a crime?

She lifted her head and met his bright blue gaze, which was fixed on her with far too much intensity for this early in the morning.

"It's not polite to stare." Especially when the look felt so much like a physical touch. It just wasn't right. "I haven't even had my morning caffeine yet," she grumbled.

He seemed less than impressed. "I have been up for two hours."

"Good for you." So, he'd gotten up at five-thirty? What a masochist. "Only, normal people wait to visit others, *especially when they neglect to call ahead*, until after eight, sometimes even nine."

His brow quirked in that sexy way he had. "We have already established I am no average man."

"Being extraordinary in no way gives you leave to be rude." But she had to admit that this man would probably get away with a lot more than she would allow anyone else in her life.

And that did not bode well for the outcome of the discussion coming.

"This from the woman who hung up on me yesterday."

"I said goodbye."

"You refused to discuss Cole's proposal in any way resembling a rational manner."

"Maybe I'm not rational, but then I live alone with no personal obligation to anyone. I can insist on keeping my home as it is for no other reason than because I want to."

"Are you going to offer me coffee?" It was a clear tactic to change the subject, but she was not fooled.

Neo wasn't convinced. Not by a long shot. The man didn't know what it meant to give up. His nature wouldn't allow it.

Foreboding skittered along her nerves as she spun on her heel without a word. He could follow her to the kitchen, or not. His choice.

He followed. The sound of his confident tread behind her further emphasized her certainty that he expected to get his way.

She poured two mugs of coffee from the pot that she had set up on the timer the night before. "Cream or sugar?" she asked.

"No."

She handed him his mug and then doctored her own with a liberal dollop of half-and-half and two teaspoons of sugar.

He was frowning at her when she looked up.

"What? I have no need to prove my masculinity by drinking black coffee."

"That is good, since you are entirely feminine." His frown deepened. "Do you often answer the door wearing nothing but a silky robe that clings to your every curve?"

She stared at him in shock for a full minute before gathering her thoughts enough to answer. "One, I am wearing pajamas under my robe."

He snorted.

"I am," she insisted. And then undid the robe that had reminded her of the beautiful blue-green depths of the ocean off Hawaii's shores to prove it. "See?"

She'd bought the pajama-and-robe set when she'd realized she probably would never see the warm waters in person again. Who would she go with? She didn't like traveling alone. And she was no longer traveling for her music.

His green eyes narrowed dangerously as she revealed the matching camisole and shorts she slept in. She didn't know what that was all about, but she was on a roll and not about to stop now.

She recinched the robe and glared up at him. "Two, I don't have enough curves to speak of to worry about such a thing." That at least should be obvious to him. "Three, I only answered the door *after* looking out the window upstairs and recognizing your car in the drive."

"News flash, Cassandra, I am a man."

"That's hardly a secret." She didn't know what was bugging him, but honestly right now, she couldn't expend the energy or brainpower to figure it out. She was too busy trying to hide her reaction to his presence…. "The point is, I never answer the door to strangers, in my robe or otherwise."

"Do you answer your door to your manager in your robe?"

Where were these questions coming from? "Of course not. Bob always warns me ahead of coming over and I am therefore not caught unawares before my caffeine or morning ablutions."

"Good."

She barely suppressed the urge to roll her eyes. "I'm glad you approve. Now drink your coffee quietly for a few minutes and let me wake up sufficiently to argue with you."

"Are we going to argue?"

"Are you going to insist on changing my home?"

"Yes."

At least he was honest.

She headed for the door. "As you are obviously not going to let me drink my coffee in peace. I'm going upstairs to shower and change. I will be back down when I feel more able to deal with you."

"Get there fast. We leave for my office in less than thirty minutes."

"You can leave whenever you like, but I have no intention of rushing my shower, or any other part of my morning regimen."

"I am not sitting down here and cooling my jets for three hours while you make yourself presentable."

"Do the women in your life really take that long to get ready in the morning?" No wonder the man got a little cranky. She'd be annoyed by that kind of time-wasting, too.

"Are you saying you do not?"

"I own exactly two types of makeup, mascara and tinted

lip balms, what do you think?" She liked stylish clothing, but it didn't take any longer to put on than jeans and a T-shirt. And if she was in a hurry, she pulled her hair back in a French plait, even if it was still wet.

"I think you now have five minutes less than you did to get ready."

"I'm not going to your office, Neo." That was so not going to happen.

"The installers will be here at eight-thirty. You can stay and supervise them, or you can come with me."

She stomped up to where he leaned negligently against her countertop and poked him in the chest, looking way too edible for a man she wanted to strangle. Only figuratively speaking, of course…mostly.

"Contractors are not tearing my house apart, Neo. It is not going to happen. If one of them so much as tries to trim the lilac bushes, I will call the police." And then her manager and fire him for getting her into this mess.

After he came over and got rid of the strangers from her home. She was never giving piano lessons away to the charity auction again.

She might have muttered that under her breath because Neo gave her an amused, if increasingly exasperated, look.

"We are going to discuss this rationally." Neo caught her hand with his, sending the rational thought he was so sure she wasn't capable of right out the window. "After."

"After what?"

"After you shower and dress." He should be angry.

She was.

But he looked perfectly calm, even somewhat tolerant, and more than a little amused.

She should be berating him for his assumption, but her

throat had gone dry and her mouth didn't want to form words. It wanted kisses. His kisses. The thought caught her up short. What was the matter with her?

Asking herself didn't miraculously present her with answers or renew her fading grasp on reality. She really wanted to be kissed by him and that was so astonishing, she wasn't sure how to handle it. She didn't know where the urge came from, but it was there. And it was strong.

He was so close. She wanted him closer. Mere inches separated their lips. How many?

"Ten inches," she guessed aloud.

"What?"

"How far," she said before she thought and would have bitten her own tongue in reprimand, but she was too busy simply trying to keep it still.

"How far what?" he asked, looking both confused and yet like he might have a glimmer what she was thinking.

"Never mind." She wanted to look away, but couldn't make herself do so.

She'd lamented the fact of her loneliness, the fact she would probably never have a family of her own. But never having been plagued with desires to kiss or touch another man, she'd also come to terms with her lack of sensuality.

Now she had to wonder, if she simply had never met the right man. She had never met Neo.

"What is ten inches?" he asked in silky demand.

And somehow she could not help telling him. "The distance between our mouths."

He didn't ask why that mattered, or laugh, or look at her like she was deranged. He didn't do any of those things. He simply lowered his head, closing those ten inches in slow-motion intensity, and then his lips were covering hers.

Shock coursed through Cass, seizing her to immobility. Neo Stamos was kissing her. And it was wonderful. More than wonderful, it was amazing, fabulous, stupendous.

Her first kiss.

Pure, unadulterated pleasure washed over her in one tropical warm wave after another. Neo's lips were firm and all male as they moved confidently against her own.

She could smell his aftershave, an expensive musk that made her knees turn to water. Or was that the feel of his tongue teasing at the seam of her lips, requesting, maybe even *demanding* entrance?

She moaned, loving the alien feeling of his tongue on her lips. The sound of his jacket rasping against his shirt as he put his arms around her sent a shiver of alien need shimmering through her. It was not a sound she had heard very often in her life, never in this context, and certainly she had not expected to hear it with him. It brought home the reality of their circumstance as his lips on hers did not.

They were too delicious. Too tingle-producing. Too amazing. Too outside her realm of catalogued experiences.

But the sound of the fabrics moving against each other was more mundane, easier to comprehend and proof positive she was indeed being held by him. Neo Stamos. The most utterly gorgeous man she had ever met, or seen even. The feel of his suit trousers against her silk-covered legs was something else altogether.

His hands roamed over her, caressing her back and hips through the thin, slippery fabric of her robe. When his large, strong hands cupped her backside, she whimpered against his mouth, her lips finally parting of their own volition to let him inside.

He deepened the kiss immediately, his mouth laying

claim to hers with both the skill and strength of a seasoned campaigner. If this was how he kissed all his women, no wonder he had a different one on his arm each night.

Even the thought of the revolving door in his bedroom could not dampen her ardor. She'd never known anything like the passion escalating inside her. She wanted to devour him. She wanted to be devoured by him. She wanted everything she had never had and so much she had never even thought about before.

What she got was a skilled mouth taking her to heights of pleasure while sure, steady hands kneaded her backside, dipping between her legs to barely caress the apex of her thighs. She cried out into his mouth at the slight touch. Naked. Yes. Naked would be good.

Only she couldn't make herself break the kiss long enough to say so. And the tiny, still-functioning part of her brain was grateful.

No part of her was happy when he tore his lips from hers though.

"No. Don't stop," she pleaded.

He set her away from him, his expression so intense, she shivered from it.

CHAPTER FIVE

HE FROWNED, not appearing in the least bit happy. "I should not have done that."

"Why?" She'd liked it, but maybe he hadn't? No, he'd been enjoying himself, or doing a wonderful job of faking it.

From everything she'd read, that wasn't the man's job. To fake it. Of course, women weren't supposed to do that, either, but some did. She wouldn't have to. If they made love. She was certain of it, regardless of the fact that she'd never actually had any practical experience in that regard.

She recognized a master when she met one and this man was a master at the art of touch. And kissing.

He blew out a long breath. "We are friends."

"Friends don't kiss?" she asked, not entirely conscious of the words coming out of her mouth, but truly confused nonetheless.

"I do not know. I have never had a female friend."

"That makes two of us."

"You have never had another woman as a friend?" His tone said he didn't think she was telling the truth.

"I've never had a billionaire tycoon friend. We are even." Well, maybe not entirely.

Female friends, or not, the man knew *a lot* more about women than she knew about men and what made them tick, billionaire tycoons or otherwise.

"So, friends can't kiss?" she asked again, going back to the part of the conversation that most interested her.

"No."

"Why not?"

"Women I have sex with rarely last more than a night, a few at the most, in my life. I would like our friendship to be more long-standing." He actually managed to sound almost vulnerable.

"We were kissing, not having sex. Weren't we?" Maybe she hadn't recognized foreplay when she felt it? She certainly wouldn't have said no if he'd asked for more and she had wanted them naked, hadn't she?

Oh, goodness, gracious, *she had wanted them naked.*

"You are so innocent."

"And you aren't. That sounds like a good combination to me."

"Only in your ingenious mind."

"Now you're just being condescending."

"I am being realistic."

"I think I might like you spontaneous better."

"Good." The look in his eyes said anything but.

"Good?"

"What could be more spontaneous than spending the day together?"

"We're back to that, are we?"

His smile said they were indeed. "You need to take a shower. I will prepare your breakfast while you dress."

"You can cook?"

"I did not start out life a rich man."

"Granted." But she hadn't considered what that might mean practicality-wise about how he lived earlier in his life.

"Do you prefer a hot or cold breakfast?" he asked, managing not to sound like a waiter taking an order so much as a superconfident Greek man trying to sound like one.

"A toasted bagel with peanut butter would be fine." She'd grab an apple on the way out the door and round out the meal nicely.

Which meant she was considering leaving with him. More than considering it, resigned to it. Maybe not even resigned, but actually looking forward to it. After a single kiss. She was in so much trouble.

Maybe his no-kissing rule for them was a good idea, after all.

"If they cut so much as a leaf off of my bushes, I will never forgive you," she said as she walked out of the room and hoped he realized she was very serious about that one.

Neo felt like someone had kicked him in the chest.

Kissing Cassandra had been better than anything he had felt in a long time. Maybe ever. He had not wanted to stop, had felt helpless to do so. That shocking realization, more than anything—more than the knowledge that Geary's team would be arriving soon, more than Neo's own pressing schedule— had given him the impetus he needed to break the kiss.

Neo was never helpless. Had not once in his entire life considered that word applicable to himself. And he was not about to begin now. Almost as alarming, he could not remember the last time he had lost control sexually or any other way, much less so quickly.

When he'd touched her lips, he'd been close to climaxing and that had *never* happened, not even in his youth. *From a kiss.* He hadn't even touched Cassandra's small but tempting breasts, or gotten to naked skin at all. But he'd wanted to. More than he'd wanted to be on time for his morning meeting. Damn it.

She hadn't touched him, either, except to respond to his kiss with her lips. That response had been untutored—innocently sensual, but incredibly, sweetly passionate. If his instincts were right, and they usually were, she was a virgin.

Which was one very good reason to steer clear of sexual intimacy with her. It had nothing to do with the fact she engendered such a surprising reaction in him. Neo was not afraid of anything, but he only slept with women who understood the expectations going in, experienced women who would not mistake physical desire for more ephemeral emotions.

His sex partners usually shared his jaded view of sex, but not much more. Women he would never consider spending an entire day with, not even in bed. Damn, he sounded like a chauvinist, even in his own mind.

But he could not help that he had never developed friendships with the fairer sex. He didn't usually make friends at all. As Zephyr had pointed out with such relish.

Neo couldn't say what drew him to Cassandra. All he knew was that the last few weeks, he had looked forward to his piano lessons and seeing her more than he ever would have expected. There was no denying he liked her as a person. With all her quirks, she was charming.

He liked how she seemed to identify with him on a level

only Zephyr ever had before. She knew what it was to have a childhood in name only. She understood loss and fear and hunger, even if it had been for love rather than food.

Her friendship was all too important. He wasn't about to jeopardize it for something as fleeting as sexual attraction. No matter how overwhelming.

He found the bagel she'd requested and started it toasting. He called Cole's cell phone while he waited for it.

"Geary Security," the other man answered on the first ring.

"She agreed to the substantive changes to the structure of the house, but doesn't want the foliage touched."

"That doesn't surprise me."

"It doesn't?" It sure as hell had stunned Neo. If it had been him, he would have had the opposite reaction.

"I researched her house's history after dropping off the proposals. Her parents bought that house before she was born," Cole said. "From the size of most of the bushes, I'd say someone planted them soon after her parents moved into the house. If I had to guess, I would suggest it was her mother."

"So, it is a sentimental thing?" Not something Neo had much experience with, for with all the luxury now at his disposal, sentimentality was still something he could ill afford.

"That's what I'm guessing, but they really do provide too much cover for burglars or stalkers."

An image of Cassandra's expression before she'd swept out of the kitchen played in Neo's mind's eye. "She's not going to let that sway her."

"You persuaded her to go for the doors and windows. You can convince her about the foliage. I'll reschedule the gardener when you do."

Neo wished he was as confident, but for the first time in years, he considered the possibility he'd met someone as stubborn as he was. In fact, the last time he remembered doing so, he'd befriended the man and ended up eventually making him his business partner.

There was only one word to describe Cassandra when she came downstairs, dressed for the day in a navy blue pantsuit.

Cranky.

She sat down to eat her bagel with a grudging thank-you tossed in his direction, the hapless bagel getting a glare before she took a resounding bite.

"You look nice," he complimented. "I like the bright pink accents." Most women he knew preened under directed praise.

And he did like the pink scarf and shoes she'd added to the more basic white blouse and dark pantsuit. Her oversized pink-and-white earrings were a nice, if unexpected touch, too.

Cassandra didn't so much as smile, though he received yet another perfunctory, "Thanks."

"I am surprised you wear so many bright colors."

He got her full attention with that comment. She glared at him. "Why?"

"I would think you wouldn't want to draw attention to yourself." "Debilitatingly shy" did not equal "vibrant dress style" in his mind, but then he was no psychologist.

"What, you think I should dress only in shades of gray and wear my hair in a bun, or something?"

"No." But he wouldn't have been surprised if she had, knowing what he knew about her hermitlike ways.

"I'm not fond of talking to strangers."

That was one way of putting it. Agoraphobic was another, but he didn't say a word.

"That doesn't mean I want to dress like a piece of cheap office furniture," she huffed and then grimaced. "It's important to me not be a caricature. I don't like to perform, but I *can* leave the house. I'm uncomfortable meeting strangers, but I don't need to dress like a hermit with no fashion sense. My life has enough limitations, I take pleasure where I find it and I happen to like bright colors."

"I'll remember that."

"I can't imagine why you'd need to."

Come to that, he couldn't, either. She wasn't one of his pillow-mates that he bought gifts for in lieu of giving anything of himself. Hell, who was he kidding? He planned to give more of himself to Cassandra today than he had to anyone in a long time. He intended to give her his time.

Still. "Now, you're just being argumentative for the sake of it."

"You think so?" she asked in a tone so subtly snarky he couldn't help but be impressed.

And amused, though he was far too intelligent to let that show. He *should be* irritated. He'd cancelled all but his most pressing meetings and cleared his schedule in a way he hadn't done in years. He would still work some, but he planned to entertain Cassandra. After all, it was his fault she was being evicted from her house for the day.

When he told her so, her frown grew slightly less dark, but it was still in the black range on the color spectrum. "I suppose you expect me to be grateful."

"Is that likely to be on the menu anytime soon?"

"No."

She was so refreshingly honest. Once she'd got past

seeing him as a stranger, he didn't intimidate her like he did almost everyone else. Again, he had an unexpected urge to smile, but he smothered it. "I'd settle for you being happy."

"Why on earth do you care if I'm happy, or not?"

"I don't know, but I do. Chalk it up to friendship."

She sighed and looked more frustrated than annoyed. "The thing is, I have obligations, too, Neo. The music for my next album isn't going to write itself. Only I can't work on it while strangers are tearing apart my house."

"So, we both take an unexpected break. What is one day?" He ignored the fact that him saying such a thing would be considered anathema by any and all who knew him.

She opened her mouth to speak and then closed it, looking at him contemplatively. "When was the last time *you* took a break?"

That was easy. "My first piano lesson."

"Before that?" she asked with a degree of consideration that made him nervous. Though he didn't know why.

"I don't take breaks."

Now she would use that truth as an excuse and say she didn't need time off, either.

She surprised him by asking very seriously, "Ever?"

"Ever."

"You *do* need a break."

So Zephyr and Gregor insisted. "If the number of compositions you have created in the past years is any indication, so do you."

That seemed to startle her. "Music is my life."

"According to both my doctor and business partner, that attitude is not a healthy one."

"I exercise."

He remembered seeing her home gym when showing Cole Geary around her house. "So do I."

"I eat right."

"So do I."

"Then why are they so concerned for you?"

Neo shrugged. "Got me, but if it's bad for me to be so obsessed by Stamos and Nikos Enterprises, then it stands to reason your single-minded pursuit of music needs tempering."

"I don't want to spend the day being dissected by strangers."

"Not going to happen."

"Why?"

"They'll be too busy watching me in wonder."

She laughed at that as he'd meant her to do. "It makes me cranky to think of my house getting torn up."

"It won't be torn up. Cole gave me his word that you'll barely be able to tell they were even here."

"How is that possible? I saw the list. They can never get it all done in one day."

"In fact, they can."

"Money talks?"

"In even more languages than I do."

A smile played at the edges of her lips. "I'm fluent in Mandarin, Italian and German."

"You are accomplished." He himself spoke Greek and English, of course, but Japanese and Spanish as well. "I understand the Italian and German, considering your passion for piano composition, but why Mandarin?"

"I like the way it's written."

"You are fluent in the Kanji?"

"Yes, though I'm still studying. I have a pen pal from

the Hunan province and he tutors me. He's a scholar and something of a recluse."

"What do you write to him about?"

"Music, what else? He plays and composes on the *guzheng*. It's kind of like a Chinese zither. Unlike the older and more traditional *guqin*, which only has seven strings and no bridges, it has sixteen to twenty-five strings with movable bridges. He can create complicated and very beautiful compositions on it."

She was babbling. She was still nervous about leaving with him and letting the security company do their job. But she was going to do it. He was proud of her.

"How do you share your music?"

"We both have Web cams." She laughed, but it didn't sound like she found that funny. "It's kind of pathetic, but I see more of him and my other online friends via the Internet than I do anyone else."

It was unfortunate, not pathetic. One day, he would help her make that distinction. "Have you ever wanted to visit him in person?"

"Yes."

"Naturally, you have not gone."

"I would. Though not easily, I *can* travel anonymously, but I have no one to travel with."

"So, it is not simply leaving your house that bothers you?"

She lifted her shoulders in a half shrug before turning back to her breakfast without answering.

He wasn't done with the subject however. "You don't like being recognized as Cassandra Baker, the renowned pianist and New Age composer."

"Something like that."

"But you wouldn't answer your door to the locksmith."

"No."

"Why?"

"My father used to say I was debilitatingly shy."

From her tone, Neo guessed the other man had considered that a liability, most likely to his brilliantly talented daughter's career plans.

"Were you always shy?"

"My mother said I was an outgoing toddler. That's how they learned I was a musical prodigy. I was always trying to entertain them and discovered the piano at the age of three. I played music I had heard from memory."

"That's amazing."

"That's what my teachers said."

"They started you with a teacher at age three?" He could not help the appalled shock in his tone.

"Mom came down sick and I guess my parents saw the lessons as a way to divert my attention from her so I would not demand too much of her time."

"That would imply you spent significant time each day playing piano."

"I did."

"How much time are we talking here?"

"I don't remember exactly." Though something in her expression belied that claim.

"Take a guess."

"A couple of hours every morning and evening before bedtime."

"Impossible."

"Entirely possible. And that does not count the time I spent practicing on my own."

"You must be mistaken." Children often miscalculated the length of time spent doing something, or so he had heard.

"I used to think I might have been, too. However, I found the records of my lessons in a box of papers after my father's death and there it was in black and white."

"What?"

"Proof my parents did not want me around."

"That is a harsh assessment."

"How did you end up in an orphanage?" she asked challengingly.

"My parents both wanted something different from life than being a parent."

"Harsh assessment, or reality?"

"Touché."

"I have often wished I hadn't found those records. I preferred the gentler fantasy that I mistook the number of hours I spent working on my music before I was old enough to go to school." She bit her lip and looked away, old sadness sitting on her like a mantle. "Cleaning out the house of my parents' personal possessions was supposed to be cathartic."

"Who told you so?"

"My manager."

"And was it?"

She laughed, another less than amused sound. "Define cathartic. It forced me to face my loss, to accept that they were gone and never coming back. Which was good, I suppose." She met his gaze again, remembered pain stark in her amber eyes. "But it hurt. Horribly."

"I am sorry."

"Thank you."

"Enhancing your security will not make them any more gone," he felt compelled to point out.

"I know."

"But making the changes is bringing back those traumatic feelings, is it not?"

She nodded, but clearly forced herself to brighten. "You're pretty perceptive for a business tycoon."

"Figuring out what makes people tick is half the battle in business."

"And I bet you are good at it."

"Stellar."

She laughed, this time sounding much happier. "Egotistical?"

He smiled in response. He liked making her laugh. "Honest in my self-assessment. Like right now, I know I'll get damn short if I'm late for my teleconference."

"Can you call in from your cell phone in the car?"

"Yes, but until I have my computer in front of me with the information I need, I won't feel good about my input."

"I bet you have most of it memorized." But she got up from the table, gathering her dishes.

"I don't like making mistakes."

"I'd lay another bet that is an understatement." She put the dishes in the sink. "Just to show I respect your schedule, I'll leave these for later."

He ignored the jibe. He respected her schedule, he just wanted to route it for the day. "I gave up betting when a careless wager led to me taking piano lessons."

"Should I be offended?" she asked.

"No. I don't regret being forced to accept my gift. It brought me a new friend."

She shook her head, but her lips were curved in a small smile. "Some birthday pressie."

"I think he did mean the lessons to be something special for my thirty-fifth."

"He really thought you wanted piano lessons?"

"I wanted to learn to play when we were younger, but I hadn't thought of that pipe dream in years."

"Not such a pipe dream anymore."

"No, but even more than that, I'm a huge fan of yours. Though I didn't know it."

"You didn't know it? This I've got to hear, but not while it will make you late."

An hour later, still reeling from the knowledge Neo was a closet fan *and* now considered her a friend, Cass listened to her latest self-recording on her MP3 player and took notes on what was lacking in the composition. She hadn't been exaggerating when she told Neo she had work to do, too, but her implication she could only do it at home might have been stretching the reality of the situation.

She didn't want to spend all day, every day, at her piano bench, so she had started working on self-recordings early on. She loved the flexibility her tiny MP3 player gave her. She could listen to it while exercising, cooking or practicing her Kanji writing. Or sitting at a table in an empty conference room in the Stamos & Nikos Enterprises building in downtown Seattle.

She'd bought her first one on the recommendation of another musician she knew online and had upgraded with each new technological advancement.

A tap on her shoulder alerted Cass to someone else's presence.

She pulled one of the speaker buds from her ear and looked up. "Yes?"

"Mr. Stamos wanted me to make sure you have everything you need to make you comfortable." Miss Parks,

Neo's personal assistant, lived up to her voice and attitude over the phone.

Blonde, in her forties, she wore her pale hair in a sleek chignon and dressed in a female power suit by Chanel, but it had to be from a previous year's collection. Because this year the designer had gone whimsical, adding ruffles and lace that would look out of place on the businesswoman. Just as the polite query sounded out of character on her tongue.

Miss Parks clearly felt offering refreshments to her employer's piano teacher was beneath her.

However the woman had absolutely nothing on Cass in the "annoyed nearly beyond endurance" stakes. While Cass sat in a strange conference room, in a huge office building filled with strangers, even more strangers were tearing *her* house apart.

She didn't even attempt to hide her bad temper when she gave the blonde a curt, "Water would be nice."

Never mind tea. That might soothe her and she didn't feel like being soothed.

Without another word to the snarky PA, Cass put her speaker bud back in her ear and returned to work. A bottle of water and a glass with a slice of lemon showed up at her elbow a few minutes later.

Bad mood or not, Cass remembered her manners and looked up to give the deliverer a polite thank-you, only to clash eyes with a man every bit as overwhelming presence-wise as Neo.

Even if she hadn't recognized him from publicity photos, she would have known he couldn't be anyone but Neo's business partner, Zephyr Nikos.

CHAPTER SIX

THE clearly charismatic Greek smiled. "No problem."

She yanked her headphones out of her ears. "Um…"

"I'm glad to get the chance to meet you in person." Zephyr's smile would have been lethal if she hadn't been inoculated that morning with a kiss from Neo Stamos. "Neo isn't your only fan around here."

She put her hand out. "Thank you for buying the piano lessons, Mr. Nikos, and I'm glad you enjoy my music."

"Zephyr, please. And don't thank me yet, you've only given Neo a few lessons." He leaned against the dark solid wood conference table. "The jury's still out on what kind of student he'll make, but my gut tells me that if he sticks with it for the full year, you'll earn every one of the hundred thousand dollars I donated to charity on his behalf."

Cass let her lips tip in a wry half smile. "I'm sitting here working from my MP3 player instead of my piano because he's got a team of construction workers and security personnel tearing apart my home. I'm under no illusions he'll be an easy student to have." Or friend for that matter.

"They're replacing a few doors and windows, that is hardly tearing the place apart," Neo said from behind Cass, his tone chiding.

She pushed her chair back and looked at him over her shoulder. "Are you done with your meeting?"

"I am." He raised a single dark brow at Zephyr. "I thought you had a full schedule this morning, Zee."

The other gorgeous Greek shrugged his broad shoulders. "I had a minute and I decided to meet the reclusive Cassandra Baker."

"It's hardly a public appearance," Neo said, sounding borderline irritated. "She graciously agreed to spend the day with me while they do necessary security work on her home. She is not here for your entertainment."

She hadn't exactly been gracious, but she appreciated Neo's minor prevarication on her behalf.

"Don't worry, I didn't have a baby grand moved into Conference Room B for an impromptu concert," Zephyr mocked, clearly amused by Neo's protective stance.

"If you had, I might have gotten more done," Cassandra joked. "There are limits to what I can do working off my recordings."

"You can afford to take some time off work," Neo said with a perfectly straight face.

Zephyr laughed in clear amazement, his expression one of disbelief. "Coming from you, that's standup comedian material."

"I cancelled several events on my calendar today."

"I know." Zephyr gave Cass a strange look. "It's one of the reasons I wanted to meet this wonderfully talented lady. I knew she was a master pianist, I didn't know she was a miracle worker."

"More like a whiner," Cass said self-deprecatingly. "Neo would never have gotten me out of my house and those workmen in if he hadn't dragged me himself."

She didn't mention his form of persuasion had included a kiss that had about melted her brain.

"You are not a whiner." Neo had come to stand by Zephyr and his expression was more than a little stern. "You have agoraphobic issues that have to be addressed with the seriousness and caution they deserve."

"That sounds like something you'd read in a textbook on the subject," she said. And then realization dawned. "You've researched my condition."

"I had one of my top people do it for me."

"Wow. You take being my student way more seriously than anyone else has in the past."

Neo shrugged, but Zephyr appeared anything but non-chalant at the admission. He was once again staring at his business partner with blatant incredulity.

Then his expression morphed and he turned a look of almost pity on Cass. "Watch out. When he gets the bit between his teeth, Neo has a tendency to take over."

"You think I haven't noticed this trait?" she asked with no little amusement.

Neo crossed his arms and frowned at Zephyr. "I think you've got better things to do than stand around gossip-ing, *partner*."

"Are you going to try and deny you've already got a recovery plan in the works for Miss Baker and her agora-phobia?" he asked instead of taking the hint.

"My research has not reached that point yet."

Cass's heart pounded in her chest. That "yet" was *ominous*. "Just because you talked me into upgrading the security on my home, do not for one minute think you are going to convince me to go through one of those antiphobia seminars. It's not going to happen."

She'd been there, done that and had the scars to prove it.

"You've tried such a thing?" Neo asked perceptively.

She nodded shortly.

"And it did not go well?" he added.

"I still refuse to answer the door to strangers, don't I?"

"That's just intelligent caution," Zephyr said approvingly.

She smiled gratefully at him. Very few people had ever tried to make her feel more normal. The people in her life were mostly vested in getting her back on the stage and that meant making sure she understood just how different she was. *Different* being one of the kindest terms they used. *Broken*, *foolish*, *weak*, and *irresponsible* were some others.

"I'll want details from the attempts you have made to overcome this challenge in the past."

"You're kidding."

"I assure you, I am not."

"Neo doesn't have much of a sense of humor." Zephyr shook his head like he pitied the other man.

Which she noticed made Neo's jaw clench and he turned a less-than-pleased look on his friend.

Zephyr put his hands out in the universal *What, me?* gesture. "I'm only speaking the truth."

Neo did not appear mollified. "I'm going to show you just how little a sense of humor I have in a minute."

Zephyr pushed away from the table and headed to the door. "Ah, reduced to threats. My job here is done." He looked back at Cass. "Nice to meet you, Miss Baker."

"Cass, please."

He grinned. "Nice to meet you, *Cass*."

"It was a pleasure to meet you, too."

"Have fun on your day off." Zephyr winked at Neo.

Neo flipped him a rude hand gesture.

Cass gasped and started laughing as the conference room door closed behind the departing tycoon.

"I apologize. I shouldn't have done that in front of you."

Cass was still smiling when she shook her head at Neo. "If you can't tell, I'm amused, not offended. I liked watching the interplay between you."

"Why?"

"It shows a side to you I don't think you exhibit elsewhere."

"What if it does?"

"Tit for tat. You want to know and have already made efforts to discover stuff about me I don't usually share with strangers, or anyone for that matter."

"So, you think you should know similarly personal things about me?"

"Exactly."

"You drive a hard bargain, Cassandra."

"I must. I got you to take time off work, even if that wasn't my intention."

"Yes. And speaking of, the rest of my morning is clear."

"You plan to entertain me?"

"I do."

"That's not necessary. I do have my MP3 player and a pad to take notes on," she admitted with some shame for her crankiness with him earlier. "And this room is nice and quiet, no distractions…well, except your business partner."

"He bought me my first CD of your music. In fact, he

bought all of them for me over time. I am embarrassed to admit I never checked for the artist so I could buy them myself, though I listen to your music daily."

"That explains how you could be a fan without knowing it."

"Yes."

She shook her head. "I love music, as you know. I can't imagine not trying to find out who created and played music I enjoy."

He shrugged, but it was obvious he meant it when he said he was embarrassed by his oversight.

She reached out and squeezed his forearm. "Hey, I don't have a clue who designed and built my house, but I bet you know."

"It was part of the security consult report."

"I skimmed that bit."

"Are you trying to make me feel less idiotic?"

"Definitely, because you aren't even sort of stupid. Is it working?"

"Yes."

"So, you took the morning off." That still boggled her mind, but she'd decided that morning he needed the break he was so determined she take.

She wasn't going to backslide and let her fear of being in the way stop her from encouraging him to leave work behind for a little while.

He nodded. "I thought I might take advantage of your undivided attention and that we could go shopping for my piano? Since both are available."

"I see." She bit her lip, considering whether or not she could psyche herself into going shopping with the man.

If she wanted to get him out of the office, she'd have to.

It didn't promise to be a pleasant morning for her, but if they stayed out of crowded malls, she should be able to manage her anxiety levels.

And he made her feel safe, like being with him she could do things that normally were beyond her comfort zone.

"Online."

"What?"

"We can retire to my penthouse and do the shopping online," he explained.

"Really? You don't mind? But honestly? You should always test out a piano before buying it."

"Do you think if I had an employee buy the instrument that I would have gone to test it out before purchase?"

"Um, no? But since you have put yourself under the aegis of my expertise, I will have to insist on it. However, we can narrow down our external shopping trip through visiting Web sites and making a few phone calls."

He looked pleased with her for some reason. "That sounds good."

She stood up. "Lead the way."

Before he had a chance to open the door, it swung inward and his PA stood there. "Mr. Stamos, I have Julian from Paris on the line in your office."

"Handle it."

"But, Mr. Stamos—"

"I told you, I am taking the morning off."

That caused the blonde to give Cass a frown that turned into a death glare when she noticed the untouched bottle of water on the table.

Cass grabbed the bottle. "I'll just take this with me."

"I have water in my penthouse," Neo said, sounding bemused.

"There's no sense wasting it." Miss Parks had been annoyed enough at having fetched it for Cass in the first place.

Though Zephyr had delivered it, Cass didn't want any more black marks in the other woman's book than she already had.

Neo put his hand out, indicating Cass should go ahead of him. "Whatever makes you happy."

The PA's already stony expression went positively sour. "Do not keep Julian waiting, Miss Park."

The older woman nodded and left without another word.

"You call your personal assistant Miss Park?" Cass asked.

"That is her name."

"It surprises me that you use surnames with each other."

"She's worked for me for six years and that's always been the way she's preferred it." Neo didn't sound like he cared one way or another.

"Do all of your employees call you Mr. Stamos?"

Neo frowned. "Yes, I suppose. Why?"

"Does Zephyr's personal assistant call him Mr. Nikos?"

"No. Again, why?"

"You keep people at a distance more than he does."

"Just because Zephyr doesn't think I make friends, doesn't mean I don't. I made friends with you, didn't I?"

If he considered steamrolling her into making substantive changes on her house as making friends. But that wasn't really being fair to him, either. "Yes."

"You sound uncertain. I thought we'd already established we are becoming friends."

"We are."

"But?"

"You're a pretty forceful kind of guy, aren't you?"

"You do not get to where I am being a pushover."

"No, I don't imagine that you do."

"That does not mean I always have to have things my own way. I'm taking piano lessons, aren't I?"

"Yes." And he'd taken the morning off when he *never* took time off so that she would be comfortable. Steamroller, or not, Neo had the makings of a *good* friend. "Where is your penthouse?"

"At the top of this building. Zephyr and I share the top floor for our living quarters."

"Considering the size of this building, your apartments must be huge."

"Part of the penthouse floor is taken up with the pool and workout facility."

"You have a pool?"

"Zephyr and I share it."

"Wow. I've thought about having one installed in my backyard, but then I wouldn't have much yard left and I'd only get to use it a few months out of the year."

"Seattle's climate isn't conducive to year-round outdoor living," he agreed.

"Not like Greece."

"Living here has its compensations."

"I'm glad you like it here."

"Yes?"

"Yes, I wouldn't have a new friend otherwise."

He grinned, his expression nothing short of pleased. "Just so."

"Still, I envy you the pool."

He laughed warmly. "Finally, something my billionaire status makes you want to have."

"You've got enough people wishing they were you."

"Are you saying I don't need another fan?"

"Oh, I'm a fan all right." Especially of his kisses, but she was nowhere near outrageous enough to say so.

"I am sure."

"I mean it. You're a great guy."

That startled another laugh from him, though she couldn't imagine why. "You cannot know what a refreshing attitude yours is for me."

"Thank you. I think?"

"Definitely. As for the pool, you are welcome to come use ours anytime you like. I will make sure you get a keycard for our top floor."

He couldn't know how tempting that offer was. She loved to swim, but public pools were more than mildly daunting for her. Or perhaps he did, considering the research he'd done on her condition.

Regardless, it was more than generous and not a gift she would dismiss on any level. "Thank you."

"Not at all. What are friends for?"

She was smiling as she followed him to the private elevator that serviced his and Zephyr's offices and penthouse floor.

Finding the piano turned out easier than Cass expected. She hit it lucky with her first phone call. She'd called her own supplier with little hope they'd have something in stock locally, but they had just taken a Steinway baby grand in as trade on a new, bigger Irmler parlor grand for another professional pianist who lived on Bainbridge Island.

"It's something of an extravagance, but the price and immediate availability are very tempting," she told him after the initial phone call. "And you've got the space in your sitting room."

Neo's apartment was huge and although it had obviously been furnished by a professional, it was pretty minimalistic—almost sparse.

"An upright would be considerably less expensive."

"Yes, but not equivalent in tone or performance. That is your standard by which you judge a monetary outlay, right?"

"More or less. Yes."

"If you're serious about learning the piano, you may as well practice on an instrument of true quality."

"You are seduced by this piano's pedigree."

"Maybe a little. A Steinway isn't to be sneezed at and it really is a bargain."

"You're very animated. I like seeing you like this."

She felt herself blushing.

He shook his head, but smiled. "Is it available to test out like you want?"

"We can go by their showroom and try the piano out today anytime."

He looked at his watch. "Where are they located?"

She told him the address in west Seattle, which was admittedly closer to her home than his building downtown.

He nodded. "If we go now, we can make it back in time."

"I thought you took most of the day off?"

"I did, though I still have a meeting later this afternoon."

"It won't take that long."

"I did not think it would."

"Then what do we have to be back in time for?" she asked in confusion.

"Lunch. It will be ready at eleven-thirty."

"Isn't that early?"

"I eat breakfast at six-thirty and you ate only an hour later."

"I'm surprised your nutritionist doesn't have you snacking midmorning with a later lunch."

"Normally, you would be right, but today is special."

Because he was taking it off?

"How did you know I use a nutritionist?" he asked. "I don't remember mentioning that."

She shrugged, tucking her cell phone back into her purse. "Lucky guess. Keeping yourself fit would be top priority and what you don't have time to do yourself, you would pay for."

"You can't do business from a sick bed."

"Oh, I'm sure you can. Furthermore, I'm sure you have."

"Not as effectively. And Zephyr goes all Greek patriarch on me when he finds out about it."

"I bet you do the same to him."

"Naturally. I can take care of whatever needs seeing to, but Zee stubbornly refuses to see that and get proper rest."

"And he feels the same when you are ill."

Neo just shrugged.

Cass grinned. "You're two peas in a pod."

"We just know who we can rely on."

"Each other."

"Yes."

"No one else?"

Neo didn't answer, but she didn't need him to. It was obvious. They were two men who had learned early not to give their trust easily. Which made the fact Neo saw himself as her friend and had offered her a key to the top floor of his building even more amazing.

She could not remember feeling so accepted, not even with her parents. Maybe especially with her parents.

Neo had never been in a store like the one Cass took him to.

It was located in a converted Victorian house. The entire

ground floor had been remodeled into a showroom for the wind instruments and pianos the company sold. The interior designer had done an outstanding job of creating an environment that showed off each instrument to its best advantage. And the acoustics had been enhanced with subtly engineered ceiling panels to maximize the splendor of sound the instruments made.

He was given a sample of the result when Cass picked up a flute, and after wiping the mouthpiece with a cloth provided by the salesman, played a mesmerizing melody that froze Neo in place.

When she was done and put the flute down, he cleared his throat. "I thought you didn't like to perform."

She blushed, looking around at the almost empty store. "That wasn't a performance. It's only the flute."

"It was beautiful."

"Thank you, but I was just messing around."

Interesting. "I thought you only played the piano."

"I dabble on the flute, is all. I wanted to learn the guitar, too, but my parents discouraged it." She brushed her hand over the flute. "They thought I should keep my focus."

"If that's dabbling, I wonder what you would have achieved with a little less focus on the piano."

Cass's smile was nothing short of beautiful. "Thank you. I love the sounds a flute can make."

"I think under your hands, any instrument would sound amazing."

She shook her head. "Flatterer."

"Not at all."

"I love music."

"It shows in your compositions."

"You really listen to my CDs?"

"All of them. Don't ask me to pick a favorite though because no matter how many times I listen, that changes almost daily."

She blushed and turned away, toward the glassed-in, soundproofed room that held the piano they had come in to see.

He followed her. "Surely you are used to such compliments."

"Actually, no. One of the side effects of my not performing is that I don't hear from many of my fans. And when I did perform, my father and manager made sure I spoke to the big money music aficionados, but not normal people who listened to my music just to make their day a little brighter."

"We have already established I do not define normal."

"But you are nothing like the *patrons* I was told to cultivate, either."

"No, none of them became your friend."

She shook her head. "A Greek tycoon for a friend. Who would have thought it?"

"It only matters that I did."

"Too true." She grinned.

"You get letters though," he surmised, going back to the original topic as they stepped up onto the platform where the baby grand piano rested.

Cassandra slid onto the piano bench, her hands caressing the piano as if it was a dear friend she was meeting for the first time. If that made any sense. "Some. Fans only have my CD label's address to send them to. Someone there answers fan mail and passes the letters along to me a couple of times a year."

"I suppose the demand for your music speaks for itself."

"That's what I tell myself."

"Do you miss it?"

She looked up at him, her amber gaze taking his breath away for a second. "What?"

He swallowed, forcing down a reaction that was not acceptable. She was his *friend*. "Performing."

"No." She shuddered, a look of true revulsion coming over her features.

"You didn't enjoy it at all?"

"I hated it. The only thing that kept me sane was the music itself."

"But—"

"I wanted to be home with my mother, not on the road with my father, or more often with a minder. I knew she was ill and I was terrified every time I left on a trip that I would not see her again."

"You knew she was dying? At such a young age?"

"Yes." There was a wealth of pain in that single word. "Like any child, I had my own sense of logic and it told me that if I was there, she could not die. I was wrong." Cassandra shook herself. "Performing for groups of strangers that were allowed to fawn over the child prodigy afterward, saying things they never would have said to an adult performer, I never forgot how much I hated it. Even after Mom died and my dad travelled with me to all my concerts, my earlier feelings colored the experience."

"He pushed you to keep performing."

"Even when Mom got very, very, *very* sick. Just as I'd always feared would happen, she died when I was on tour in Europe. I was seventeen. They didn't tell me until two days later—my father put me off when I tried to phone her.

She'd been so weak, I believed him when he said she was resting every time I called. I felt selfish asking her to call me, like it would tax her waning strength too much."

CHAPTER SEVEN

"THAT is monstrous!" Neo wanted to hit something, but there was nothing to hit and no one to yell at for the sins committed against this woman. "Why would they do such a thing?"

"They didn't want to spoil the last performances on the tour. My father and Bob said I owed *all* my fans the best I was capable of."

He cursed in Greek. Colorfully.

Cassandra's lips twisted in a near smile. "Exactly. My father channeled his grief into my career."

"Where did you channel yours?"

"Into the music."

"But you hated it."

"Not the music, just the concerts."

"So, when he died you stopped torturing yourself."

"That's how I saw it. My manager does not agree."

"Naturally not."

"Bob thinks I'm hiding from my parents' deaths by surrounding myself with their things."

"Isn't he the one who convinced you to get rid of their personal things?" And why the hell was the man still her manager?

"Yes, not that it made a bit of difference in my desire to go on tour."

"Not the catharsis he was expecting then."

"All I know is that the idea of getting on a stage in a packed concert hall makes me want to throw up."

"Do not worry. I will not ever ask you to play for me and I will ensure Zephyr does not, either."

Her mood changed with a flash and nothing but pleasure glowed in her lovely amber gaze. "I wouldn't mind playing for you."

His knees wanted to give, whether it was from the shock of her offer or the effect her clear happiness at the thought had on him, he did not know. Hiding the momentary weakness, Neo slid next to her on the bench at the Steinway. "You would play for me?"

"What are friends for?" she asked, tossing his own words back at him and making him smile.

"I would like that very much."

"Then consider it done." She grinned, all shadows gone from her features for the moment. She tipped her head down and looked at him shyly through her lashes. "I didn't know if I would want to, but I do. In fact, I look forward to it. I used to really enjoy playing for my parents."

But no one else, or so her words implied. "I am honored. It is something I will look forward to with great anticipation."

Smiling, Cassandra concentrated on the instrument in front of her. She looked to check that the door was shut on the soundproof room and then played a short piece, not any music he recognized, just a series of chords. Her head was cocked as if listening for something he couldn't begin to hear.

It sounded fine to him. More than fine.

"Well?" he asked, when she sat in silence for several seconds after the keys fell silent.

"Try your scales on it."

He played the keys as she'd taught him at the first lesson.

"Now, try a few of the chords you've learned."

He did.

"What do *you* think?" she asked.

"It's good?" he asked in uncharacteristic hesitation.

"Did the keys feel natural, not clunky?"

He considered and then nodded. "They felt fine."

"A baby grand really does have better key play than an upright, but nothing can compare to a concert grand like I have. I'm spoiled, but this is a nice instrument." She patted the top of the Steinway.

"What you are saying is that it is not as nice as yours though."

"Buying a Fazioli for a beginner would be an excessive extravagance and you told me you don't squander money indiscriminately. Besides, their waiting list is a long one."

"A Steinway isn't an extravagance?" he asked with a quirk of his lips.

"Not at the price they're offering it."

"So, we *are* getting a deal?" he asked, making no effort to hide his relish at the thought.

"I told you we were. A very good one." She told him how much they would be saving and even he was impressed.

"I knew bringing you with me would be a benefit."

She laughed and shook her head before playing a simple

children's tune as if her fingers could not stay still that close to a well-tuned instrument.

He caught the salesman's eye through the glass and waved the man over.

Neo handed the salesman a black American Express card when he entered the soundproof room. "We'll take it. You can arrange delivery with my personal assistant. Here is my business card. Call this number and it will go directly to her line."

"Very good, Mr. Stamos. We'll arrange a piano tuner to accompany the movers so it is ready for use directly after delivery."

Cassandra nodded her approval and Neo said, "Fine."

The salesman left with Neo's American Express and business cards, but neither Neo nor Cassandra moved to get up from the piano bench.

She brushed her fingertips along the keys. "It's been a few years since I bought a new instrument."

"Getting the urge?"

"To replace my Fazioli? Never. But I might be persuaded to buy some new music for my flute."

"So, you decided you could afford to play a second instrument."

"I dabble, like I said, but sure, why not? If I can learn foreign languages and make time for Tai Chi, why not play a second instrument as a hobby?"

"Zephyr says I have no hobbies."

"Don't worry." She patted his back consolingly. "You have one now. Playing the piano."

"Yes."

"Let's work on some chords."

"Here?"

She looked around the soundproof room and the mostly empty showroom beyond. "Why not?"

"Isn't that like performing?"

"No one can hear us in here."

"You're addicted. That's what this is about, isn't it? You miss your piano?"

"I'll make a deal with you. You learn two chords and I'll play a short piece from my newest score for you."

"Here?" he asked again, inelegantly.

"Where else? It's soundproof in here and we can close the drape over the window for extra privacy. And we can't exactly go back to my house."

"We could, but I'd prefer you not return to the scene of the crime until the last bit of sawdust has been vacuumed up."

"Scene of the crime is right."

"Stop whining and show me a chord."

He couldn't believe how much he enjoyed learning the chords she wanted to teach him. No one bothered them. Not even the salesman, who came in quietly only to leave the receipt and paperwork for Neo's purchase on top of the piano, and then left just as quietly.

"Okay, I think I've got it," he said after playing the chords successfully several times. "Now, it's your turn to keep your part of the bargain."

"You got it." She got up and closed the drape on the window then tugged on the door to make sure it was shut.

She returned to the piano bench. She didn't ask him to leave it and he was curiously hesitant to do so. So, he stayed.

She started to play a piece he recognized from one of her early albums. It was a particular favorite of his and he sat quietly while she played it *just for him*. It wasn't a long, or complicated piece, so it was over all too soon, but he would cherish the memory of that impromptu entertainment for years to come.

She looked sideways at him. "That was just a warm-up."

She really was going to play a new piece. Again *just for him*. Her fingers danced across the keys, coaxing gorgeous sounds from the Steinway and he knew this new CD would be one of her best yet.

When she finished she looked up at him and smiled. "It's nice, isn't it?"

He didn't know if she meant the piano or the piece, but he said, "Yes," to both. "Thank you." He looked down at her, hard pressed to refrain from following his gratitude with a kiss.

She tilted her head back and met his gaze, her amber eyes glowing with joy from the music and something he could not define. "You are welcome. That was the first time I've ever played in a public place and enjoyed it."

The showroom wasn't exactly a concert hall, but he was proud of her for keeping her end of the bargain all the same. "Glad to be of service."

"You make me feel safe."

He was lost for words.

She blushed and ducked her head. "Isn't it about time we got back for lunch?"

"I'm sure it is." He tipped her face up so their eyes met. The moment was too profound to ignore. "Thank you."

"I…"

"I have rarely in my life been as honored as I am by your trust in me." His head tilted forward of its own volition.

She let out a soft puff of air. "Are you going to kiss me again?"

"Not a good idea."

"Why?"

"We are friends."

"And friends cannot kiss." She smiled and pulled her chin from his hand, clearly trying to lighten the atmosphere between them.

He would do his part. "I have never kissed Zephyr."

"Liar."

That made him reel back. "I have never kissed a man."

"That whole kissing on the cheek thing you Greek guys do? What's that?"

"Oh." Heat climbed the cheeks she mentioned. "That is not the same." At all.

"No, but it's still a kiss."

"You are walking a dangerous path, *pethi mou*."

"Pethi mou?"

"Little one." His little one, but he didn't need to tell her that bit.

"I'm not that little."

"Compared to me?"

"You're just oversized."

"I thought that was my ego."

"O-ho, so you have perturbed a girlfriend, or two."

"I've never had a girlfriend, but yes, more than one pillow-mate has remarked that I have a rather healthy ego."

"I'll bet."

"I will tell you what I tell them—it is deserved."

"And do they agree?"

"Naturally."

She bit her lip, looking away from him, that adorable expression he could easily become addicted to on her features. He liked Cassandra Baker shy. He wondered if he should tell her.

Not everyone thought she had to perform publicly to be valuable.

"I've never had a boyfriend, either," she whispered, breaking in to his thoughts.

"Never?" That should not have shocked him, but it did. He had guessed she was a virgin, but to be wholly innocent of male-female games? He could not imagine it.

"Um…no."

"How old are you?"

"Twenty-nine. I'm a real freak, aren't I?"

"What?" He grabbed her shoulders and made her meet his eyes by sheer force of will. When her amber gaze was looking into his, he said, "You are precious, but are you saying this morning was your first kiss?"

"Well, actually, um…yes."

Oh, hell, didn't his libido just love that? "I wish I'd known."

"Why?"

"I would have made it special."

"It felt pretty special to me."

"It could have been better."

"How?"

"It's not something I can explain with words."

"Novelists do."

"I'm a businessman, not a writer. I'll have to show you."

"Here?" she squeaked.

"Yes." He covered her lips with his before she could get another query out.

Gently. More carefully than he had ever kissed another woman. Even his first time. But damn. The knowledge no other man had done this battered at his vaunted self-control. However, he would not give in to the mouth-ravaging his own desires demanded.

Her lips tasted every bit as good as they had that morning, but the knowledge they were his and no one else's added a sweetness he had never once thought to experience. A sweetness so real, he could taste it as certainly as he did the unique flavor of Cassandra's delicious mouth.

Of their own volition, his arms slid around her, pulling her so close their body heat mixed. She felt right in his arms. Too right. Like she fit exactly as if she had been made to be held exactly as he held her.

He refused to dwell on that sensation of rightness, choosing instead to enjoy this anomalous moment in time. His tongue swept through her mouth, claiming her as only he had ever done.

His body demanded he claim her in other ways. Thankfully they were in a semipublic setting, or he might not have had the strength to deny himself.

This being friends with a woman was harder than he had ever expected it to be.

Her slender fingers tunneled into his hair, short-circuiting rational thought. Cassandra kissed him back with an unfettered sensuality he knew would be a joy between the sheets.

She had never kissed another man, but she knew exactly how to tease his tongue into her mouth. Her feminine instincts were rock solid as she dueled with his tongue while making whimpering sounds of need that drove his libido through the roof and beyond.

Damn. Damn. Damn.

He was seriously considering pulling her under the piano and away from prying eyes when the sound of a near tortured squawk had him yanking his head back.

He reared up and looked around only to see that the door to their soundproof room stood open. The salesman must have thought to speak to them only to get an eyeful when he opened the door.

Through the doorway, Neo could see a young boy blowing determinedly into a clarinet. The source of the awful noise. The child's mother was staring at Neo and Cassandra with a sappy expression that had Neo jumping off the piano bench.

That woman's look screamed, "Romance…isn't that sweet?" He didn't do romance. Not even for Cassandra.

He put his hand out. "Come. We'll be late for lunch."

"Don't forget your paperwork," she said, though her eyes indicated she wanted to say something entirely different.

Lunch was a banquet of Mediterranean cuisine. It had started with *fasolada*, the bean soup Cass had always associated with Greece. Then there had been a small salad made up of leafy greens, pine nuts and crumbled feta with a dressing unlike anything she'd tasted before.

"This is amazing," Cass said as she scooped a bite of the main dish, spinach *spanakopita*, onto her fork. "There's no way you eat like this every meal."

"Naturally not. But today I have a guest. My housekeeper was thrilled I told her not to worry about the nutritionist's directives and to prepare a traditional Greek meal for you. She is from the Old Country and she does not approve of my nutritionist's directives, to say the least."

And far from bothering him, Neo seemed to enjoy the Greek woman's attitude. Cass would bet her new flute music that his housekeeper was an older woman and that what she fed him wasn't the only thing she fussed about.

Neo had found a way to have a mother without the emotional baggage of a close relationship.

Cass waved toward the table with her fork. "This is a feast."

"I'm glad you are enjoying it."

"I fell in love with Greek food when I played in Athens."

"You played in Athens?"

"Yes. When I was twelve. It's a beautiful city."

"I agree, though I couldn't wait to see the back of it when I was younger."

"I'm sure it looks different to you now than it did to the orphan boy who left it behind."

"Very much so."

"Do you and Zephyr return often to Greece?"

"At least once a year, though always under the guise of business. We have never taken a vacation there."

That wasn't saying much. "You don't vacation at all," she chided gently.

"Neither does Zephyr."

"So, you are both workaholics."

"And you? Are you a composeraholic?"

"Making up words now?"

"Why not? Scientists do it all the time."

She couldn't help laughing. "Zephyr said you don't have a sense of humor, but I think he's wrong."

"That is only because his sense of what is amusing borders on the insane."

"You are lucky to have each other."

"He is the brother of my heart."

She stared at Neo for several seconds before saying, "I'm surprised to hear you say something like that."

"Why?"

"I don't know. It sounds so sentimental, I guess."

"Truth is not sentimentality," he said in a tone that left no doubt he was offended.

She stifled a smile. "Well, I'm glad you have that truth in your life."

"You do not, do you?"

"What do you mean?" But she knew. It wasn't something she liked to think about.

"You had parents, but they were taken from you long before their deaths by your mother's illness and your father's choices."

She couldn't deny his observation, but agreeing with it would hurt too much so Cass remained silent.

"And now, you have no one you would call family."

How true. Online friends could fill her free time, but not the heart's need for proximity relationships. And her agoraphobia prevented her from developing those. Oh, she made friends on occasion, certainly more frequently than Neo seemed to.

But eventually all those she would call friend got fed up with her limitations and either moved on, or turned into what she considered martyr friends. Those people that wouldn't dump her because of her issues, but who so obviously wished they were elsewhere when they were with her.

She was determined to enjoy every moment of her friendship with Neo.

But even with that resolve, the loneliness of her life rose up and slapped her emotions a stinging blow. However, she made herself shrug noncommittally. "I have friends."

"None that you trust as I trust Zephyr."

"I never trusted my parents as much as you trust him. And I wouldn't have trusted siblings that way, either." Maybe. It helped her to believe that right then.

"You cannot know that."

She should have known he would call her on it. "You're correct, of course. In fact, don't laugh, but my favorite daydream as a child was that I had brothers and sisters who loved me for me and not because I could play a piano the way I do."

"There is nothing in that to make me laugh." He reached across the table and cupped her cheek. "Know this—our friendship does not rely on your playing piano."

And even though she was his piano teacher and he was a fan of her music, she believed him. "Thank you."

"We have two hours until my next meeting, is there something particular you would like to do?"

"Do you watch movies?"

"It is one of my guilty pleasures."

She grinned, internally shaking off the negative thoughts their conversation had produced. "A movie then."

He showed her his collection and she discovered that Neo had another secret besides the stock that made up his portfolio. The man liked old movies. The classics. They watched a film starring Spencer Tracy and Katharine Hepburn, both laughing in all the same places.

When it was over, Neo had to return to his office for a meeting. "You can stay up here if you like."

"Thank you, I'd like that." She sighed. "I wish I'd known you had a pool. I would have brought my suit."

"Zephyr and I keep a selection of swimsuits in the changing room for our female guests. I'm sure you could find one to fit you."

"Are you serious?"

"Yes. They are replaced each spring with a selection of the season's new styles."

"I suppose for a couple of playboys like you, that's not a wasteful expenditure."

"It has come in handy a time or two," he admitted without a single blush.

"I bet." It took her a second to realize the emotion she was feeling was jealousy, but she refused to acknowledge it. She did not have that kind of a claim on Neo, even if he had kissed her. Twice.

"You can access the pool through that door. You'll have to prop it open with a chair because it locks automatically when it closes. I'll have a key made for you to access this floor, but it won't open my apartment, or Zephyr's."

So, his trust of her only extended so far. No surprise that. The only true shock was that he trusted her at all. She shook her head at him. "You've got a real thing about locked doors, don't you?"

"Safety first."

She cracked up.

Amusement still showed on his face when he left.

She found a burnt orange bikini that fit as if it had been made for her and changed into it. If the sexiness of the cut might tempt Neo to further kissing extravagances, who was she to argue? Who was she kidding? Neo wasn't about to be tempted by her not-so-curvy form.

She still liked the swimsuit. It made her feel sexy, even if maybe she wasn't exactly femme fatale material. And she found she felt perfectly comfortable at the thought of Neo seeing her in it. Even if it didn't tempt him to mind-melting kisses.

The pool was the perfect temperature and she swam several laps, enjoying the unlooked-for treat.

She was sitting on the side, dangling her feet in the wet and drinking water from a bottle she'd found in the pool bar's fridge when Neo returned.

He looked harried.

"Tough meeting?" she asked.

"I am regretting my choice in contractors."

"That's not a feeling you have often, I'm sure."

"You're right. I weigh my choices carefully and I thought I had this time, too."

"What happened?"

"He had done two smaller projects for me before, but despite his claims to the contrary, it is now obvious he does not have the resources for this much larger one."

"I'm sorry to hear that."

"He'll be far sorrier if I have to fly out there."

"Where is it?"

"Dubai."

"Really? I've always wanted to go."

"I'll make a deal with you—if I go, I'll take you."

She rolled her eyes. "Yeah. Thanks."

"Are you afraid of flying?"

"Flying? No. The crowds in the airport and on the plane are enough to give me nightmares." Though she could deal with them if she had to. Maybe.

"What about a private jet?"

"I've never flown on one."

"It is the only way I travel. For both expediency and security reasons."

Wow. She leaned back and smiled up at him. "Of course you have your own jet."

"Well?"

"Well what?" She thought she should know what he was asking, but it was escaping her.

"Would you like to go to Dubai with me on my private jet if the project ends up requiring my personal supervision?"

"I…" Was he serious? He certainly seemed so. "You…" The prospect was so tempting. She missed travelling so much and she could not imagine a better partner for doing it. She couldn't imagine anyone else making her feel comfortable enough to be so tempted. "I think so, yes."

"Fantastic." And he looked like he really meant it. Like he was proud of her.

She bit her lip, blinking back tears. He was an amazing man. And the trip sounded wonderful. But best of all, she would be with Neo. That was even more tempting than the travel. "I've never thought to try flying private."

She could have rented a private jet to fly her domestically at least, but the thought had never occurred to her, even when she used to jokingly lament about the lack of private railcars nowadays.

"We'll have to give it a test. Before Dubai. Go somewhere not too far away. Maybe a trip to Napa Valley."

"Are you kidding?"

"I don't have a sense of humor, remember?"

"I know that's not true."

"Well, I am not joking."

CHAPTER EIGHT

"But there's nothing in it for you." And wouldn't such a trip require him taking even more time off from work?

Her head was reeling and so was her heart.

"Helping my friend with her desire to travel is something."

"You're crazy."

"I do not think so."

She laughed, feeling happier than she had in years.

"Besides, I like California wines. I wouldn't mind a chance to visit some of the better vineyards and purchasing some of their selective stock."

"Hmm…"

"Do you like wine?"

"I don't drink."

"Religious reasons?"

"No. It's just…I'm a lightweight."

"How light?"

"I smell the cork and I'm tipsy."

"This I should like to see."

"And when I start making words up to go with my instrumental compositions? So not pretty."

"I would like to hear you sing."

"No, you wouldn't. Trust me. As talented as I am on the piano, I am conversely as horrible a singer."

"You only increase my desire to hear it."

"You're a masochist? I never would have thought it."

"And if you had, you would have been wrong, but I like the idea of hearing you be less than perfect."

Implying what? That he thought she was mostly perfect? Now that wasn't possible. With her problems, no one thought she was perfect. Or even close to it. "So you can laugh at me?" she teased.

"Laughing *with you* is surprisingly pleasurable."

She remembered the movie and nodded. "It is."

"So, you will sing for me?"

"If we go to Napa Valley and if you convince me to taste some of this selective wine you plan to buy, you just might get that treat."

"I'll hold you to that."

"There were a lot of ifs and maybes in there," she warned.

He shrugged as if the only words he knew or heard were *yes*, *can* and *do*. "Are you all swimmed out?"

"I could do a few more laps."

"Then, I will join you."

"Great." That's just what she needed. The most gorgeous man she'd ever met running around in a swimsuit.

After the two kisses today, her body was going through all sorts of palpitations and excitations. She wanted to grab him and throw him on the deck beside the pool and kiss him until both their lips were sore, but he said friends couldn't kiss. And he wanted to be her friend.

He'd already shown that meant something real to him. Friendship. He'd been there for her when she needed him and he'd never once chastised her for her weakness. He'd given her his time today and she knew that was something special.

Neo Stamos was a dream man. If only her limitations weren't so redolent of a nightmare.

She wasn't going to do anything to mess this relationship up before it ran the natural course all her other friendships had over her life.

Seeing him in his swimsuit was worse than she expected. Neo was clearly not ashamed of his body. Showing his European upbringing, he wore spandex swim trunks that showed off his stomach and thighs like no California board shorts could ever do. It wasn't a Speedo, having a little leg to it. But it was enough to make her whimper as feelings she had read about, but never personally experienced before meeting him, zinged through her body.

"Did you say something?"

She had to clear her throat. "Uh, nothing. Nice suit."

"It creates minimum drag when I am doing laps."

"Of course." She thought he'd just bought it to seduce unwary virgin pianists. Well, maybe not.

They swam several laps, even racing a couple, which he won.

"It's just because I wore myself out swimming before you came up." It didn't help that she had a hard time concentrating on her breast stroke when all she wanted to think about was what Neo would feel like pressed up against her as he had been at the piano showroom.

Only wearing nothing but swimwear. Not that she was about to admit that out loud. Still, she shivered in the heated water at the yummy picture her mind presented her yet again.

"Ah," he said sagely. "It's got nothing to do with the fact I'm more than a half a foot taller than you with more powerful leg muscles?"

"Let's leave your leg muscles out of it." She scrunched her face at him. "You'll give me a complex."

"Your bird legs are quite lovely."

"Bird legs?" she screeched. Had he seriously called her legs birdlike? "What is that? Scrawny and orange?" Oh, he was so going down. She shot under the water, diving for his ankles.

Whether it was surprise or simply good timing, she managed to get her arms around his ankles and yank, pulling him under the water. Not being an idiot, she let go immediately and bolted to the other side of the pool as fast as she could swim. She was half out when big hands clamped onto her waist and lifted.

She went sailing through the air to land with a splash in the center of the pool. She had the presence of mind to hold her breath as she went under, but still came up spluttering. *And* ready to get her own back only to find him waiting for her, a devilish smile on his too handsome face.

This was fun. Really, really fun. She hadn't played like this in, well…ever. In just five weeks, Neo had given her so much. Her heart was so full, she felt it might burst.

At the last second, she checked her instinct to grab him and try another dunking. She couldn't help noticing that Neo stood firm, his head and most of his shoulders above the pool line while she had to tread water to keep her face out of it.

"You think you've won?" she demanded breathlessly.

"I think we're even right this minute," he said with obvious concession.

She mock growled at his taunting, but said, "A smart woman would leave it at that, I suppose."

"A draw is better than defeat," he acknowledged.

She gave him a really good glare and sent a wave of water cascading toward him. "You're so sure I would lose?"

With hardly a blink at the deluge that broke over his head, he wiped the excess water droplets from his face and shrugged. Definitely his confidence was unquestionable. And totally justified. Unfortunately.

"You might be bigger, but maybe I'm more devious," she posited.

"Highly doubtful." He grinned. "I'm a real estate developer. I deal with devious every day."

"You've got me there." The music industry could be cutthroat, but she stayed out of the business side as much as possible.

"Can I sweeten the *draw* with an offer of refreshments?" he asked.

Why did the word *draw* sound so much like *defeat*? "What kind of refreshments?" she asked, tempted despite her newly awakened sense of competition.

"Macadamia nut cookies and baklava. My housekeeper was *very* happy to have her normal restrictions lifted."

Cass's mouth watered and any thoughts of futile attempts at a second dunking for the big man flew from her mind. "You've sold me."

"I'll meet you inside."

Only if she could get out of the pool after nearly drowning herself when she forgot to keep treading water while watching his muscular backside walking away from her toward one of the shower enclosures.

* * *

Neo heated the water for tea to go with their pastries and reminded himself of all the reasons he could not bed the sexy woman still drying her hair in his guest bathroom. Hell, he'd come close to making love to her in the pool. Then on the deck when she'd stepped out of the water.

He should never have looked back before closing the door on the shower room. She'd had a glazed look in her eye he associated with things not remotely related to swimming.

But damn did she look delectable in a swimsuit. Supermodels would kill for a body so well-toned. Cassandra wasn't anorexically thin like those women. Thank heaven. No protruding bones in places where at least a minimal layer of insulation should reside.

But the only things that jiggled were supposed to. Even if her curves were modest, they were mouth-wateringly succulent. Petite but perfect breasts and small round globes of a bottom that tempted his hands and mouth. He had wanted to leave a love bite on one flawless mound in the worst way.

She'd almost started something very different than what she'd intended with her dunking game. When he picked her up to toss her into the pool, he'd very nearly brought her body to his mouth instead of letting her go to splash in the water.

Oh, hell. What had he been thinking suggesting she use the pool?

That she'd wear one of the more modest one-pieces he knew could be found in the changing room. That's what. Absolutely not that she'd choose to swim laps in three tiny triangles that revealed more than they hid. The damn bottoms were almost a thong. And Cassandra had a perfect butt.

Luscious. Well-rounded, but clearly the result of time spent in her exercise room because…damn. Perfect. Yes, that was the only word that fit. And the lack of tan line indicated whatever sunbathing she did, she wore a suit of similar construction.

His heart could barely take the strain of thinking about that one. His virginal friend was too damn sexy for either of their sakes.

Hearing the continued sound of the hair dryer just made him want to go in there and offer his services helping her dry those glorious, silky tresses. What woman in today's age grew her hair to her waist like Cassandra had? Didn't she know it took too much work for a modern woman to maintain?

He nearly laughed at his own musings. Apparently, Cassandra had not gotten the memo.

He'd had no idea how long the soft brown curtain was until he'd seen her braid as she sat beside the pool. It hung down the middle of her back, the tail brushing enticingly against the top curve of her backside. He had immediately wanted to see what the brown silk would look like fanned out on his pillow, or hanging down around both their faces as she rode him to ecstasy.

His eyes slid shut, the pain of unabated arousal humming through him as he bit off a Greek word even he didn't say very often.

He grabbed his phone and dialed.

Zephyr picked up on the second ring. "What's up?" he asked in Greek.

"Remind me why it's a bad idea to have sex with your friends."

"Did I say that?" Was that amusement Neo heard in his partner's voice?

"No. I did, but I need reminding."

"What friend are we talking about? The new piano teacher?" That was definitely laughter lacing Zephyr's tone.

Neo growled, "Yes."

"I'm surprised."

"That I want to have sex with her?" He always thought Zephyr was more discerning than that.

"No, that you are calling her friend already."

"She's special."

"I see." All amusement was gone now.

Finally, the other man was taking this seriously. "Good, because I do not. Tell me to keep my hands to myself."

"When have you ever listened to me?"

"Damn it, Zee…"

"You really are in a quandary, aren't you?"

"I like being her friend. I don't want to ruin that."

"And having sex with her would do that?"

"Of course. Wouldn't it?"

"That depends."

"On what?"

"On what her expectations are going into the sex. When both people are on the same playing field, sex between friends can be more mind blowing than anything you'll experience with a mere hookup."

He wasn't sure he and Cassandra *could* be on level playing ground. "She's a virgin," he told his friend with simple honesty. "Totally innocent."

"At her age?"

"Yes, and another reason not to take her to my bed."

"Unless she's tired of being inexperienced. Are you sure her state is by choice?" he asked in a tone that implied Zephyr knew something about this sort of situation from his own experience.

"What do you mean?"

"Think about it. Cass has lived her whole life for her ailing mother and her music. I doubt her father let her date when she was younger and now she's got this agoraphobia thing going on. When is she going to meet a man she might enjoy making love to?"

"That's not the point."

"It's not?"

"No. *I* can't be that man." That was the point.

"Why not?"

"Because she'll end up hurt. She's not like my—"

"Other hookups? Maybe it's time you graduated beyond the one-night stand."

"I am not looking for a relationship. I don't have the time."

"Everyone has time for friends, Neo."

"No, they do not."

"Let me rephrase that. Everyone should make time for friends. What's the point of being at the top of your pyramid if there isn't anyone up there with you to enjoy it?"

"I have you."

"Your business partner and only friend. Hell, Neo, half the time you and I are in different countries dealing with our business."

"So?"

"So, you can't spend all your time working."

"This record is getting old, Zee."

"Is it? Or is it finally starting to sink in?"

"You know you are a hypocrite, don't you?"

"We aren't talking about me right now."

"Good thing for your sake."

"Right. Listen, does Cass want you?"

"I think so, yes." Hell, if he was wrong then somebody shoot him now, he'd lost his ability to read people.

"So, let her know the score and allow her to make her own choice."

"She might not make the one best for her."

"She's an adult, Neo. It is her call."

"You make it sound so damn simple."

"And you are letting it get way more complicated than it needs to be."

Neo didn't need Zephyr to tell him sex with Cassandra would be better than any hookup. His body had been yelling that very message at him since she'd opened her door to him the first time. In fact, he realized he didn't need Zee to tell him anything at all.

He already knew what he wanted and he damn well knew what he was going to do about it.

Maybe she wasn't his usual type, but she wasn't the Plain Jane he had first considered her. Cassandra was no supermodel.

Damn it, she was better.

She might love her bright designer fashions, but there wasn't a vain bone in her body. Her innocent sensuality was a thousand times more provocative than another woman's practiced seduction and he had the erection from hell to prove it.

Neo had never practiced self-denial when it came to sex. He met a woman he wanted, she wanted him, too, and they danced the horizontal mamba a few bars. Well, he wanted Cassandra, and he was damn sure she wanted him, too, but for the first time, that wasn't the only consideration at hand.

The blow dryer cut off. Neo's hands fisted at his sides

as he fought through an internal quagmire of conflicting thoughts. One thing shone through the rest—Cassandra Baker had spent twenty-nine years being denied aspects to life most people took for granted. First by the circumstances of her childhood and then by the limitations of the anxiety that plagued her.

He could give her a taste of passion—more than a taste, a whole buffet. Maybe friendship didn't have to preclude sex. Not if both people wanted it.

And Neo wanted it. So did Cassandra.

Cass walked into the kitchen expecting to find Neo making tea, which was such a domestic thing to do, it really endeared him to her.

What she did not expect was the feral gleam in his green eyes and the clear tension thrumming through his body.

"Are you all right, Neo?" she asked, wondering if she should have put her suit jacket back on and not sure why that particular thought was flitting through her brain.

Except for the way he was looking at her. Like her white silk blouse was transparent and the lacy bra she wore beneath it not much better.

"You left it down."

She looked to the right and then to the left, but neither the pristine counter nor the small bistro table set with goodies and tea things gave her a clue what he was going on about. "Um, okay. Did you want me to pour the tea?"

He didn't answer, his hands clenched as if he was trying to stop himself touching something.

"Uh, Neo? You're starting to worry me."

"Is it desire or lack of opportunity?" he demanded in a guttural voice.

"I don't think I know what you are talking about." In fact, she was sure of it.

"Your virginity?"

"My vir…" she squeaked, choking the word off midway. "What are you talking about?" And why were they talking about it? Being untouched at age twenty-nine was not exactly her favorite topic for contemplation.

He crossed the distance between them with two long strides. "Your innocence. Is it a condition you are pleased about?"

"Pleased?" Right. Because every woman wanted to stare thirty down without ever having had a boyfriend, much less a serious relationship. "Neo, you aren't making any sense!"

"It is a simple question, *pethi mou*."

"I'm sure it is, only I don't know what the question is." She was getting an inkling, though, and her face was flaming because of it.

"Zee said you might not be a virgin by choice, but rather by necessity."

"Necessity?"

"For lack of opportunity," he clarified.

"You talked to Zephyr about my sex life?" she asked in outrage as her brain finally caught up.

He ignored her. "Lack of sex life. If you had a sex life, my own would be so much easier."

"I don't see how."

He slid his hand under her hair to cup her nape, the gentle touch at odds with the feral gleam in his green gaze. "Don't you?"

The heat from his hand froze her vocal chords. No, that didn't make any sense. Shouldn't heat unfreeze them? But they felt frozen, unable to move. All she really knew was that she couldn't speak. She wasn't even sure why she was having the silent dialogue in her head, except that it was easier to think about that then what Neo was trying to discuss.

"I do not wish to take advantage of you." His thumb brushed her neck, up and down...up and down, sending tingles through her with each light sweep.

Her vocal chords finally unstuck. "Neo, you cannot go around discussing my private life with Zephyr." Really, really.

"I did not go anywhere. I called him from right here."

"You know what I mean."

"I know I want you."

"You do?" Okay, that bit of information was certainly enough to sidetrack her.

"Definitely."

"But what about the *no kissing friends* rule?"

"I am rethinking my stance on that one."

"Oh." Well, it was probably a good idea, considering the fact he kept breaking it.

"Hence the call to Zephyr." Where they talked about her virginity.

Oh, man. Her whole body flushed with embarrassment. "And he said..."

"That I should let you make your own choices. That you are an adult."

"He's right. I've been all grown up for years and as much as it seems to happen—or used to—I detest having others make important decisions for me. Only the problem here is that I'm not sure what I'm supposed to be choosing between."

"Sex with me."

Oh, heavens. Okay, she really got it now. "As opposed to friendship without sex?" she asked, just to be sure.

"Precisely."

"And after the sex?"

"The friendship remains."

Friendship never remained for her, sex, or no sex, but now probably wasn't the time to mention that salient little fact to him. "Friends with benefits."

"I guess." A sound of dark amusement came out of him. "Some benefit. As I told you, I have never had a female friend before."

"But you do now. And you want to make love, er, have sex with her."

A brilliant smile broke over his features. "Exactly."

"But you don't want anything else. Beyond friendship?"

The troubled expression returned. "It is not fair to you."

"Why? If it's fair to you and I do assume you think it is? Why wouldn't it be fair to me?" What made her so special?

"You are far less cynical than I. And I'm worried you will mistake our intimacy for…"

"Love?" she asked, clueing in to the fact that even in the abstract he wasn't comfortable saying the word. Never mind the obvious reality that he thought she wasn't just lacking in cynicism but was encumbered with a big dose of emotional naiveté.

"Right."

"It goes without saying you won't make the same mistake."

He shrugged one shoulder. "I have never fallen for any of the women I've taken to my bed."

"If you had, we wouldn't be having this conversation." And even the thought had the power to hurt her. Maybe she was more at risk here than she realized.

"The truth is, I don't think I'm a guy who does the softer emotions."

"Ah, you don't think you are capable of love?"

"I have never loved anyone, never been loved by anyone."

She knew that wasn't true. The affection he and Zephyr shared was love if she'd ever seen it. They loved like brothers. Like family. She hadn't experienced it but she knew what it looked like. Family love. Neo was clearly uncomfortable acknowledging the feeling but he'd been lucky to experience it.

The discussion was moot in regard to her anyway. She hadn't engendered unconditional love in her own parents, no way was it going to spring forth from Neo's manly chest in relation to her. She had never expected to be loved—longed for it, but never expected it. And it had been years since she allowed herself to even daydream about such a thing. She didn't feel as lonely when she didn't dwell on what she could not have.

And she wasn't going to let it stop her from having what she could.

"I'm not expecting love from you," she told him honestly.

CHAPTER NINE

"WHAT do you expect?"

"Nothing. I learned a long time ago that expectations lead to disappointment."

"What are you looking for, then?"

"I'm not sure I'm looking for anything. Your advent into my life was like a comet dropping from the sky, totally unanticipated and a little earthshaking, if you want the truth. Your friendship is a remarkable gift."

He took a deep breath and stepped back. "That's it then."

"But sex would be wonderful, too." Not that she thought *wonderful* even began to describe what she would feel sharing her body with this man.

"So it *is* a matter of opportunity."

"Not exactly." She hadn't dated. She'd never kissed, but she'd met men who wanted to bed her. Groupies that might be rich and snobby, but were groupies nonetheless and frankly, they'd scared her silly.

Almost as badly as getting on stage to play a concert.

Talk about performance anxiety. What would someone who almost deified her because of something she couldn't control—her talent—expect from her in bed?

"But you do want me now?"

"Right now?" she asked with an embarrassing hitch in her voice.

"Yes, right now."

"I always want you," she admitted quietly. "From the very beginning I've wanted you, even when I didn't recognize what that feeling was."

"But you recognize it now?"

"Yes." And how. It was a screaming ache inside her. And he was offering to assuage it. She could have cried with relief.

"And you are ready to act on those feelings?"

"Here? Now?" Her voice had gone high with nerves, though to be honest—yes, and *yes*.

"Do you have other plans?"

"Tea?"

He smiled, almost indulgently, though his demeanor was anything but. He looked like an ancient warrior contemplating his next conquering. "I think tea can wait."

She could do nothing but nod. Tea *could* wait. He could not. Her virginity would not. She maintained a façade of semicalm on the outside, but inside, she was shaking.

He must have sensed it because he bent down and picked her up, one arm under her legs and another behind her back. Just like always, she felt safe with him, even when faced with the unknown. He turned and headed down the hall that led to the bedrooms.

"I don't want to get naked in a bed tons of other women have gotten sweaty in." Not only did her heart—which wasn't supposed to be engaged in this—rebel, but so did her *ick* factor.

The last must be the only thing that registered with him because instead of getting all worried that she was getting emotionally carried away, he laughed. "I change the sheets or rather, my housekeeper does."

"I don't care. We can use a guest bed."

"Actually, we cannot."

She frowned up at him.

"When I bring them back to my penthouse, I don't take women to my bedroom, we go into the guest room."

"Okay, it's the master bedroom then."

"You do not mind *my* sweat?"

"We are friends."

"Ah." But he was still clearly laughing at her.

She didn't care. He could be as amused as he liked, but while she might not ever have his heart, she would demand every concession his friendship afforded.

Neo could not believe that he was carrying Cassandra into his bedroom with serious intent. The intent to share his bed and his body. His hold on her tightened as he inhaled her scent and reveled in the knowledge of what was to come.

His body rejoiced while his brain tried to wrap around the change in his circumstances. She wanted him and she understood the limitations of their relationship. Not only understood, but accepted.

Friends with benefits. He would have to discuss this concept with her. The idea she might decide to have benefits with another friend down the road did not sit well with him. Their case was a special one and she would need to understand that. Another man might not treat her gene-rosity with the respect and appreciation it deserved.

But right now, Neo was going to give her exactly what he had promised. He was going to blow her mind with pleasure.

They entered the bedroom and he turned on the light with his elbow. The California king-size bed was in the center of the room and he headed directly for it. He leaned down to pull back the top sheet and duvet, then he laid her on his black Egyptian cotton sheet-covered mattress. Her beautiful brown hair fanned out on the pillows just as he had known it would.

Reaching out, he smoothed his fingers through it. "It's like silk."

"It flies everywhere when I don't keep it put up."

"And yet you left it down for me."

She looked at him with confusion for a second, but then she smiled and nodded. "Yes, I think I did."

"You knew I craved to see and feel it."

"I did notice you looking at my braid rather intently by the pool."

"I was looking at all of you intently."

"I wasn't sure if I wasn't imagining that."

"You were not."

"I'm glad." Her smile was sweet and, for all her inno-cence, full of womanly mystery.

"As am I."

"I wanted to feel our bodies pressed close together in just our swimwear."

"I will give you better than that. There will be nothing between us."

She shuddered, her eyelids going half-mast. "I might not survive it."

"You are good for my ego." And Zee had been so right. Even the bantering with her was different…he was himself, he wanted to talk.

"Does it need stroking?"

"No," he admitted with a smile. "But it feels good nonetheless."

"I get that."

"Do you?"

"Yes. I know I have uncommon talent with the piano, but it still feels really nice when others express their appreciation."

"You do get it." She got *him* like no one else. Not even Zephyr. The warm approval in her pretty amber eyes went straight to his groin. "Yep."

"Get this," he said as his hungry mouth pressed down over hers.

Her lips gave way under his almost immediately and he took instant advantage, sliding his tongue inside to taste sweetness that was rapidly becoming addictive. Her response was complete and unhesitating. She flicked her tongue against his while her sweet lips moved with unconscious sensuality.

His body knew what to do and without even thinking about it, he started stripping his clothing away as he kept her occupied with one devouring kiss after another. He wore only his briefs when he started on the buttons of her blouse.

Her hands slid down from his head and seemed to stutter when they encountered naked skin, but within seconds she was caressing everywhere she could reach, her slender fingers mapping his torso with passionate curiosity.

He slid her blouse back, revealing her lovely body. He wanted to see, but he didn't want to stop kissing her.

She made up his mind for him by dragging her mouth from his. "You won't be disappointed?"

He reared back and looked down at her, taking in the satin smooth skin of her stomach and the worried glint in her amber gaze at the same time. "How could I be disappointed? You are beautiful."

"I am not."

"Who determines the splendor of a piece of music?" he demanded.

"The person listening."

"And who decides what is beautiful in what they see?"

She hesitated for a moment, but then grudgingly said, "The person looking."

"So?"

"To you I am beautiful, but you're just saying that."

"No."

"But…"

"You must trust my words."

"Okay."

"Okay." He used the moment of trust to pull her blouse the rest of the way off and dispense with her bra in one well-practiced series of movements.

Instead of trying to cover up as he half suspected she might, she reached up. "Come closer, I want to feel your skin against mine."

"You are perfect for me," he told her heatedly. "I adore this passionate innocence of yours."

"Passionate innocence. That's me," she said with a self-deprecating laugh that choked off into a moan when he gave her what she craved and felt the trembling result in the feminine limbs wrapped around his shoulders.

How had such a sensual woman made it to twenty-nine without having sex? Even with her lifestyle and limitations?

"That's so good," she breathed into his ear while moving from side to side infinitesimally. "So good."

"Yes, it is."

"I want my slacks off, too."

"My pleasure." And it was, undoing the crisp navy trousers and pulling them down her legs.

He had to stop and look, soak in the sight of her sprawled out on his bed in nothing but her panties.

"Incredible," he said.

She shook her head. "Now, I know you are lying. You told me I had bird legs."

"I was teasing." With a shake of his head for her ignorance, he pressed his body down onto hers, reveling in the feel of naked flesh pressed against naked flesh. "I was picturing them wrapped around my torso while I pleasured you."

"You weren't."

"I was."

"Like this?" she asked in an innocent tone, completely belied by the mischievous sparkle in her eyes. Her legs wrapped around his hips, her calves hooking over his thighs.

"Exactly like that." He took a deep breath and held it while keeping his body rigid. "Careful, *pethi mou*. I am in grave danger of reaching the goal long before the game is over."

"A Casanova like you?" she teased. "I don't believe it."

"Believe." No matter how embarrassing he might find it, that was the truth.

"I like affecting you that strongly."

"I, too, like it." And to prove how much, he began to kiss

her again. This time, caressing her with his lips all over her face and down her neck.

Her legs' hold on his hips broke as he continued his oral caresses down over her satiny shoulders and lower to her breasts.

Her breathing, which had grown rapid and shallow, hitched. "Oh, oh…Neo…yes. I like that."

He would have laughed if he had any air to make the sound, but he didn't feel like laughing when his lips closed around one delicately pink peak and she cried out with shocked delight. He felt like giving the victory chant. She was so incredibly responsive. To him.

Every one of her reactions belonged to him and him alone. As did she.

No matter how temporary his possession, it pounded through him as a primitive, fierce drumbeat. She was his.

He nibbled, suckled and licked her nipple and the soft mound surrounding it, like she was a particularly tasty ice cream cone, until she was making incoherent sounds of need. And then he moved to her other petite breast and gave it just as much attention.

Her hands went from caressing him, to burying in his hair, to pulling his hair, as she bucked her hips in an ancient if unconscious plea.

No matter how much he wanted to give in to that silent demand, she wasn't ready. Not yet. But she would be.

He was going to drive his sensual little virgin out of her mind with carnal delight.

With that goal firmly entrenched in his mind, he moved down her torso, his lips and tongue caressing and tasting the salty smoothness of her skin. She writhed under his ministrations, making incoherent demands when he tongued her belly button. His hands were busy revisiting every spot his mouth had already been.

He played with her breasts, but it wasn't until he pinched and teased at her hard little nubs that she tried to arch up off the bed. He laughed in victory-filled pleasure against her smooth stomach and slid his mouth lower. When he reached her hot pink panties, he stopped with his teeth on her waistband.

Everything in Cassandra seemed to go still. She stared down at him. Their eyes locked as he made silent promises and she reeled from the message he knew she could read in his gaze. He was going to make this the best first time she could possibly have.

She deserved the most incredible experience he could give her. She wasn't just a one-night stand; she was his friend. And her innocence was not merely a powerful aphrodisiac, it was a great responsibility as well.

With a jerk of his head, he tugged the small scrap of lace down. Blatant desire tinged by virginal uncertainty washed over Cassandra's precious features. She canted her pelvis so that he could pull off her last piece of clothing over her hips.

In other circumstances, she might be shy, but in this, Cassandra was tantalizingly open.

Pretty brown curls were revealed to his hungry gaze now that her panties were on the floor with the rest of their clothes. The natural feminine mystique was a nice change from the waxed, shaved and tweezed nether regions he'd been exposed to over the past few years.

He ruffled the curls with his fingertips and she bit her lip on a moan.

He smiled. "Sensitive?"

"Yes, but…"

He brushed his hands down her legs, stopping with them clasped around her ankles. "There are so many things your body can feel that I look forward to showing you."

"And will you feel them, too?"

She was smart, his sweet little Cassandra. "Yes. Giving you pleasure will turn me on so much I won't be able to stop—"

"Pounding into me."

The earthy words coming from her prim mouth were almost enough to send him over the edge. "You are dangerous, *pethi mou*."

"That's good to know." And indeed, she did look proud of herself. Then she dipped her head, looking up at him through her lashes in a gesture he was coming to recognize as her default in uncertainty. "You won't really pound. Not at first, will you?"

"Sweetheart, I will never hurt you. Not even accidentally. I will be so careful with you, you will beg me to hurry."

"That could be fun." Her words were all bravado, but the relief in her lovely features told its own story.

"Yes, I think it will be."

"You know what else would be fun?"

"Many things. What did you have in mind?" he asked, enjoying himself in a way he never had in bed with a woman.

"You. Naked."

"You are a delight."

"I can't tell you how pleased I am to hear that. Now, strip."

"I have already stripped, or hadn't you noticed?"

"Don't be smart. You know what I want."

"Ah, you wish equal disrobing?"

"Well, you've just got those small briefs left and they

don't look like they're very comfortable." She did her best to appear like his comfort was all that concerned her. Of course, the innocent hunger in her eyes sort of ruined that.

Nevertheless, he looked down at himself and had to agree with her assessment. His briefs did not look comfortable, not with the way his hardness was trying to press out of them. The fabric was stretched thin trying to cover the length of his rigid penis and he had to wonder how much longer they would be able to do so. Though he was not sure he wanted to remove them just yet.

Leaving them on was a mental boundary for him. The last barrier between him and the untouched channel between her legs.

Instead of answering, he stalled for time by running a hand up the inside of her thigh.

She shivered, letting her legs drift farther apart. "Everywhere you touch feels so amazing, like I've got electric currents running under my skin and your fingers are the conductors."

"I like making you feel electrified." He let his fingertip dip into the honeyed warmth of her passage and had to stifle a growl of pleasure. She was soft, silky and wet.

Everything he so desperately needed.

Neo's fingers breached Cass's vaginal entrance for the first time and her brain emptied in a red haze of desire.

Everything they had done so far was new for her, but this was in its own class. Having him touch her there made her feel like she belonged to him on a primal level. And although he was the one doing the touching, that didn't stop her from feeling like he belonged to her, too.

A wholly alien sense of possessiveness washed over

her even as she shifted again to give him better access to her most feminine place.

He touched her like he couldn't get enough and that was more stimulating than the caresses themselves. It made her feel wanted for something other than her talent at the piano. For the first time in her memory.

This was no friend having pity on the hopelessly innocent. Neo wanted her and every touch of his hand or mouth showed just how much.

As did the erection seriously tenting his briefs. She wanted to see his male member, she really did, but couldn't seem to remember how to make her mouth work to remind him of that fact. She couldn't take her eyes off his body.

He chuckled, a dark and sexy sound that only increased the arousal pulsing powerfully through her body.

"How does this feel?" He pressed one finger inside her. She wondered how anything bigger was ever going to fit because she felt stretched with that single entry.

"Full," she got out breathlessly.

"Do not worry. You will stretch to accommodate me."

"Maybe."

"Definitely."

"You're a lot bigger than your finger." But that finger felt so good.

"You'll be thankful for that later."

"I'll take your word for it," she gasped out between panting breaths as his finger caressed her interior.

He pushed a little farther inside and she felt a flash of pain. Making a noise of dissent, she tried to arch away.

"Shh...relax. This is your hymen and it must be breached for our intimacy to be achieved."

"I'm not a Victorian maiden. I know that, but it hurts."

It was unsettling the impact a little pain marring her pleasure could have on her. She would have to trust him to know what he was doing.

But she was acting on instinct, too.

"I want you inside me when the last barrier to my virginity is crossed."

"Are you certain?"

"Yes."

He smiled and nodded.

"As you wish." He got up. "I need to get condoms."

"Where are they?"

"In the guest room."

He really never had sex in here. For some inexplicable reason, Cass was really pleased about that fact. Sex in his bed was for her and her alone. The newly developed streak of possessiveness in her nature rejoiced.

He was gone less than a minute, returning with a small box that he tossed onto the bedside stand. He'd already taken one of the small, square foil packets out of it and was tearing it open.

"Watch me. Next time, I want you to do this."

"Has anyone ever told you that you're bossy?" she asked even as part of her thrilled at his instruction. It wasn't as if she wanted to look anywhere else.

"Demanding. Assertive. Pushy. Stubborn. Difficult. Perhaps bossy once or twice."

She huffed out a laugh. "I have a feeling I'll be using all those and more."

"No doubt." He pulled his hand away. "Now I make love to you, *yineka mou*." The Greek in his accent was thick and strong.

She didn't correct his semantics. She didn't want to.

Right now, for the first time, she needed to feel like they were making love. Even if it was just sex. Between friends.

And then, as impossible as it might seem, she realized in that moment it was because she *did* love him. She didn't know how it had happened so quickly, or even if the feeling was real, but she felt a depth of feeling for him she had not felt in any form since her parents' deaths.

And wasn't this exactly what he had warned her against? Mistaking sexual feelings for real emotion? Only it did not feel like a mistake. And she had to wonder if the sex could feel so good and right for her without some emotion attached.

She wasn't about to ask him, but it was a topic she would explore with some of her online friends. Ones who had more of a life than she did and might be able to give her the insight she needed.

For now, she just concentrated on how it felt to have Neo joining their bodies. It wasn't all joy and yet rather than making her irritable as she'd feared it would, the pain felt even more intimate than the pleasure.

An indelible marking on her soul that would connect her to him for the rest of her life.

Though he was slow and careful entering her, it still hurt and tears leaked down her temples. He leaned down to kiss them away and whisper soothing Greek in her ear. She didn't know what he was saying, but the tone comforted her and caressed the ragged edges of her spirit.

Once their pelvises touched, he stopped moving completely, giving her time…? She thought that must be it because the sweat beads formed on his forehead told their own story about the cost such patience had on him.

"I feel so connected to you," she whispered as their gazes joined as intimately as their bodies.

His eyes closed and he whispered what sounded like no.

"No?" she asked, unaccountably hurt.

"*Ne*. Yes," he hissed. "It is Greek."

"Oh." Good.

"You make me lose my English."

She thought that might be one of the nicest things anyone had ever said to her.

"Is it always like this?"

His eyelids lifted, revealing a gaze gone dark with passion. "No. It is never like this. Not for me."

She wanted to say something to that, but didn't know what. He was not declaring love or even an intent for something long-term; he was simply acknowledging that this moment was special. For all she knew, she was his first virgin.

"Zephyr told me it would be phenomenal." Neo's voice was strained, like the toll from remaining still was getting heavier.

"Sex with a virgin?"

"Sex with a friend."

"Oh."

"Indeed."

"But I already knew it would be like this with you."

"You did?"

"Why do you think I wanted it so much?"

"Oh," she said again, not having any other words.

He pulled out slowly, abrading torn tissues, but causing a jolt of pleasure to go through her all the same.

"Okay?" he asked.

"Yes." Maybe more than.

And then he was moving, swiveling his hips and hitting a spot inside her that sent jolt after jolt of electric sensation through her body.

"So good," she fairly groaned, though the soreness had not gone entirely. She felt a muted spiral of pleasure and she wanted more but wasn't sure how to make it happen.

He sat back and tugged at her wrist until he had her own hand placed palm down on her belly just below her belly button. He pulled until the tip of her middle finger just brushed her clitoris.

She cried out at the surge of sensation that tiny touch caused.

"Keep it there," he instructed and then he started moving again, faster this time. And with every body-jarring thrust, her fingertip caressed her center of pleasure.

That muted spiral became a tornado and she felt orgasm claim her in shattering convulsions.

Finally, she went limp from the quakes and aftershocks and only then did she feel him stiffen above her.

He yelled something in Greek as he climaxed, and then he looked down at her. "Amazing, *yineka mou.*"

She would have to ask him what *yineka mou* meant, but not right now. All she wanted to do in this moment was bask.

He quirked a brow at her, his face reflecting satiated pleasure.

"Mind-blowing."

His smile was as good as the kiss that came after it.

CHAPTER TEN

NEO lay next to Cassandra and watched her sleep. He had insisted she soak in a mineral bath after their lovemaking, and then had tucked her into bed, where he had served her a late supper instead of seducing her into round two as his body had urged him to do. Now she slept and he remained awake, shocked at his own behavior.

Since when did he pamper his sex partners, much less actually *sleep* with them?

He was not a selfish lover, but he shied away from any form of intimacy, spoiling with anything but extravagant gifts included. This friends-with-benefits situation was a dangerous thing, he realized.

Cassandra deserved a little coddling. No doubt about it. And perhaps that was all this urge to pamper, coddle and care for was about. He saw a dearth in his precious friend's life and was determined to fill it.

She'd received little enough of it in her life even though common sense might say she should have gotten more than her share. But no one in the brilliant musician's sphere had seen the price she paid for her music as anything other than what had to be done.

Her mother had been an invalid, and yet rather than giving the small child Cassandra had been extra love and attention to make up for that, she'd been thrown into a world of public performance that clearly terrified her. Worse, she'd been forced to stay there.

Neo might have grown up on the streets, with a short stint in an orphanage, but he knew that wasn't acceptable behavior for a family. He could not regret her father was dead, or Neo would be tempted to beat the man. Not that her manager was entirely safe. The temptation to destroy the man was strong, but Neo would rather focus his energies on helping Cassandra regain certain elements to her life.

Like travel.

She had seemed so excited at the prospect of going to Dubai, and even Napa Valley with him. He would never have thought she enjoyed travel so much, being as connected as it was to her public performing.

But apparently the incredibly talented pianist had found one thing to enjoy on her concert tours. Experiencing new places.

He was determined she would know that joy again.

He would look at his schedule in the morning to see when they might plan the trip to Napa Valley. It would have to be soon, because if he ended up going to Dubai, it would be in the next month. And chances were good on that trip. He wanted to take Cassandra. He wanted his new friend to experience all the delight life had to offer.

Including, but not limited to, devastating sex.

And maybe he would find her a new manager, one who

saw Cassandra as a person, not a meal ticket. Or at least was very good at pretending so.

Cass woke in a strange bed for the first time since her father died and she stopped travelling for her music. It was a comfortable bed with soft sheets and duvet of perfect weight. She could easily snuggle down and go back to sleep, a sense of warmth and safety enveloping her.

Until her brain supplied just whose bed she had woken in. Neo's!

She could still smell him on the sheets. That yummy aftershave he wore and a scent she would forever associate with sex. She reached out, but found the sheets beside her empty. They were still warm from another body, though. Neo had slept with her.

Memories of strong arms holding her, a tender kiss on her lips and a whispered "Good night, *yineka mou*" warmed her.

She could barely wrap her mind around the fact he had slept with her—all night long, much less her lascivious memories of the night before.

Sitting up in the Ralph Lauren white T-shirt Neo had lent her to sleep in, she felt only tiny twinges in muscles used so differently from her normal exercise regime. The mineral bath had helped. A lot.

She bit her lip on the smile Neo's insistence she soak in the enhanced hot water brought to her face. He'd been so sweet, but she intuited he would not thank her for saying so.

He'd taken such good care of her, but what had really surprised her was him carrying her to *his* bed after the bath. She'd assumed that if she was staying over, she would do so in the guest room. But that wasn't what happened.

He'd brought her to his bed. Without the slightest hesitation or discussion.

And though she'd never once slept in the same bed as another person, she had rested deeply, waking only once in the wee hours of the night. Rather than being bothered by the body wrapped so protectively around hers, she had reveled in the experience, knowing it might not ever happen again.

She didn't think Neo made a habit of sleeping with his mistresses. No doubt he'd made an exception for her because it had been her first time.

He really was a nice man.

"What's put that smile on your face?" the man himself asked from the doorway, dressed immaculately and obviously ready for work.

"You," she admitted.

His brows rose.

"Really. You're a very nice man, Neo Stamos, billionaire business mogul."

He shook his head. "Don't let my contractors hear you say that."

"I wouldn't dream of it."

"Dora has breakfast waiting for you when you are ready."

Cass looked around, but did not see a clock. "What time is it?"

Neo flicked a glance at his watch. "Seven-thirty."

"You look ready to go to work."

"I am. I woke late, but have a meeting I must attend."

"Can I return to my house today?" she asked, fearful of the answer. She couldn't help noticing, he had never mentioned Cole Geary calling the night before with the all clear.

"Yes, of course. Cole's team finished the installations before dinnertime yesterday."

"You didn't say anything."

He shrugged, but the skin over his sculpted cheekbones went a burnished hue. "I was enjoying your company."

"Ditto," she hastened to assure him. "I certainly don't mind, but it would be good to get back to work on my composition."

"Get done what needs doing by Friday."

"There goes that bossy gene again."

"A hazard of spending your time around business moguls."

"You think?"

"I know."

"Just so you don't expect to always get your way."

"Just so you don't expect me not to try."

She laughed, feeling more free than she had since her initial decision to stop performing. "What's happening on Friday?"

"We're flying to Napa Valley after dinner and staying for the weekend."

Shocked to her pink, bare toes, she jumped out of the bed. She hadn't let herself hope he meant it about travelling together, but hadn't he told her at least once he did not say things he didn't mean? "You're serious?"

"I've instructed my pilot to book both takeoff and landing slots and Miss Parks to rent a house for the weekend."

"All since waking up?"

"I texted them both last night, after you fell asleep."

"But it's such short notice."

"Money—"

"Talks and the rest of the world listens." She shook her head in disbelief. He gave her so much and didn't seem to even realize it. "You're amazing! Thank you!"

He accepted her enthusiastic hug without a glimmer of

hesitation, but kept his kiss swift. "I cannot afford to get sidetracked by your too-alluring lips this morning."

"You find my lips alluring?"

"Most definitely."

"Good to know." She was feeling positively giddy and it showed in her voice.

"You think?"

"Sure, knowledge is power," she said cheekily.

"So they say." His eyes travelled down her T-shirt-clad body, the heat factor increasing steadily until he gave her a look that singed her to her toes. "Know this, if I did not have to attend this meeting, I would be taking you back to bed and touching you until you screamed."

"Wow. Maybe we can try that scenario in California this weekend." Yes. Please.

"Consider it done." He took a deep breath. "I am leaving now. Do not be intimidated by Dora. She is my housekeeper, therefore not a stranger."

It said a lot about how much she trusted *him* and how comfortable she was in Neo's home that his words actually settled inside her with truth. "Got it. Not a stranger."

"Will you be okay with her driving you home?"

"Surely that's not in her job description?"

He shrugged. "I thought you would be more comfortable with her than my usual driver."

"So, you do use one."

"When necessary, yes. I like driving though."

"And you like being on time. Go."

He shook his head and then grabbed her and placed a hard, lingering kiss on her lips. Then he spun on his heel and left the bedroom.

She put her fingers over her lips. "Wow." She spun in a circle. "Just wow."

Dora turned out to be a Greek woman in her mid-fifties with salt-and-pepper hair worn in a neat bun. She had a kind smile and the apparent desire to feed the nations. The breakfast she laid out for Cass was big enough to feed an army.

When she said so, the older woman grinned. "One day That One," she said, tilting her head toward the door as if Neo were still in the apartment, "will settle down and give me some *bebes* to cook for."

The image of little boys with green eyes and dark hair teasing a sister into eating her dinner so they could all leave the table to play flashed through Cass's mind. It filled her with a longing she thought she had long ago conquered. "He'll make a wonderful father."

"Not that he knows it." Dora rolled her eyes as she poured Cass a cup of aromatic coffee. "Men!"

Cass laughed. "I don't have much experience with the species, except my manager." And Bob was less a man in her mind than the nagging voice of business.

Neo's bossiness didn't really bother her, but when Bob got overly demanding, she felt borderline bullied. One thing was for sure, if he could have cajoled her into returning to the stage, he would have done it. Goodness knew he kept trying.

He'd played every guilt card in the deck. At least twice.

"You are the pianist. Mr. Neo told me. I enjoy your music."

"Thank you."

"You will have to slow down when you have children. Two CDs a year." She shook her head.

"I doubt I'll ever have children, but I would not mind cutting back on my composing for their sake if I did."

"Why should you not have children?"

"Some people never find that special person to spend their lives with. I wouldn't wish myself on a child as a single parent, either." Not with her limitations. It wouldn't be fair to the child.

"So, you're a little shy. I've read your biography. Not everybody likes to be the center of attention. You'll make a wonderful mother. You mark my words."

Cass just smiled, hiding how much she wished the other woman's words weren't just wise, but were prophetic. Only Cass knew how impossible such dreams were in her life. "Neo said you would drive me home this morning."

"Yes. He did not think you would like going with his driver, or so he said."

"That's right. Strangers can intimidate me."

"Yes, I'm sure. It has nothing to do with the fact his driver is a very attractive young man. No. Of course not."

Cass was startled into laughter. "I do not think Neo is the jealous type."

Dora made a noncommittal noise and then told Cass to eat her breakfast.

Cole Geary was waiting for Cass when she arrived at her house.

She was amused to discover that Dora had no intention of leaving Cass alone with a man. The older woman's traditional values were showing. Cass was only surprised Dora didn't seem to think less of her for so obviously spending the night with her employer.

Cole walked Cass through all the changes, which *were* pretty unobtrusive. Getting used to the alarm system was going to be the hardest part.

"Strange to look out through a window and realize the glass wouldn't shatter if a neighbor kid hit a ball at it."

"You get used to it," Cole said.

Dora nodded. "Mr. Neo's got a glass partition around his balcony that's supposed to stop bullets. It's got to be cleaned just like any window."

"It's top-quality shatterproof material." Cole sounded proud of that fact. "The same stuff they used during the president's acceptance speech."

"He takes his safety seriously," Cass remarked.

"He has to."

Cass felt an internal shudder at that reminder. "Sometimes, I forget he's such a successful tycoon."

Cole looked at her like she'd lost her mind, but Dora's smile was clearly approving.

Once they'd finished the tour of the new security measures and programmed her palm print into the biometric locks, Cass offered the other two coffee. Cole declined due to another appointment. Dora accepted, offering to make the coffee while Cass changed into fresh clothes for the day.

As Cass was dressing for the second time that morning, it occurred to her she may well have made a second friend.

The phone rang that night just as Cass was getting ready for bed. It was Neo.

"Dora said Cole walked you through the changes."

"Yes. They're better than I expected. They even painted all my window trims the same color they were. You can barely tell the difference."

"I told you."

"It's not nice to rub it in when you are right, Neo."

"You did not mind me being right about how good intimacy between us would be."

She choked out a laugh. "Jerk."

"Seriously? You just called the great Neo Stamos a jerk?"

"I was teasing, oh, Mr. Greatness."

His laughter was rich and warm.

"Were you late for your meeting this morning?"

"Naturally not." He paused. "But I did not have time to do my usual preparations."

"I'm sorry."

"You do not sound so."

"What do you expect? I impacted the great Neo Stamos's schedule. That's pretty impressive."

"Proud of yourself, are you?"

"Absolutely."

"I feel the same."

"You do?"

"You can ask that after the honor you did me last night?"

"Was it such an honor?"

"Very much so."

"So, um…you haven't had a lot of experience, with virgins I mean."

"No, but more importantly, I have never made love to a woman who touched me like you do."

"I don't know how to touch you," she wailed, admitting one of her fears. She'd spent the day reliving the night before and one thing had become glaringly obvious; she had been the recipient, not the giver. She was going to have to do some research.

"I was not talking about the physical, but trust me when I tell you there is nothing to fear there."

"I do trust you."

"I know. You are flying to Napa Valley with me."

"You sound like I'm doing you a favor and we both know the opposite is true." For the first time in years, Cass felt like she was truly living, not just existing through her music.

"Every time you give me your time it is something to appreciate."

"Your brain doesn't work like other men."

"You are just now realizing this?"

She laughed. "Don't be annoying."

"But I am good at it. Ask anyone."

"I don't believe it. Demanding. Commanding. Brilliant even. But not regularly annoying."

"Perhaps it is a talent that only comes out with you."

"It does that. I still can't believe you kidnapped me from my house yesterday."

"Do you regret it?"

"Not even a little."

"Good."

"Will you still be here for your piano lesson next week?" she asked.

"Yes."

"I promise not to waste time on pleasantries," she teased.

"I do not."

"No?"

"No. I find it very pleasant to kiss you."

"If you expect kisses and…other stuff…you had better schedule extra time because I expect you to learn more chords."

"You are a slave driver."

"I've heard that one before and I'll tell you what I've told my other students."

"That is?"

"You bought lessons to learn to play the piano, not sit and stare at it."

"Technically, I did not buy the lessons at all."

He had a point, but she wasn't foolish enough to acknowledge it. "Zephyr would not be happy to hear his lessons were being wasted."

Neo said something in Greek and she laughed.

"I get the feeling I don't want to know what you just said."

"Certainly I do not want to tell you."

"Embarrassing much?"

"Perhaps a bit. You can take the boy out of the streets, but not the streets out of the boy."

"I don't believe that. You've come too far from your origins to see yourself as a homeless urchin in any way."

"I do not forget my beginning. It drives me to achieve more in the present."

"Will it ever be enough? The success you've achieved?"

"Funny, Zee asked the same thing recently." The bantering humor had dissolved from his voice to be replaced by something that almost sounded like melancholy.

"What did you tell him?"

"That he was just like me."

"Which is not an answer at all."

"I do not know."

She knew Neo did not mean he didn't know what he had said, but rather that he did not know if his success would ever be enough.

"I'm sorry."

"Now, you sound like you mean it."

"You should be happy with what you have done with your life, proud of yourself, but you're still striving to prove something to yourself."

"It is not something I think about."

"Maybe you should."

"Perhaps, but right now, I am too busy thinking how I am going to schedule enough time to have both you *and* my lesson next week."

"Focus on clearing your schedule for the weekend. That comes first." And he'd probably get enough of her he wouldn't feel the need to do more than study piano the following Tuesday.

Neo called the next morning to remind her to turn off her alarm system before stepping outside. He called again after lunch to ask how her current composition was going. She told him if she got it done, she would play it for him over the weekend.

She wasn't at all surprised when the phone that never rang did for the third time as she started making preparations for a solitary meal.

"Hello, Neo."

"How did you know it was me?"

"No one else calls me, except my manager and people from my CD label. None of them ever calls after five p.m. I guess they don't keep your kind of hours."

"Speaking of work hours, my teleconference call for this evening got rescheduled. Would you like a dinner guest?"

"Hasn't your housekeeper already prepared your dinner?"

"Whatever Dora made will keep."

"Wouldn't you rather eat out?" she asked and then wanted to smack herself for the defeatist behavior. He was already aware of her shortcomings; she didn't need to outline them in stark relief.

"I would rather share this time with you."

Oh, darn. Could he get any more perfect? That feeling

of love she was so sure couldn't be real so soon only got stronger. "Then by all means, come over."

"I'll be there in thirty minutes."

"I'll see you then."

He was as good as his word, ringing the bell exactly twenty-nine minutes later.

"It smells good," he said appreciatively as he followed her into the kitchen.

"It's just pasta and chicken." She picked up the serving dish and headed to the dining room, but didn't stop at the table. "It's such a nice night; I thought we could eat on the back patio. There are no shatterproof clear barriers, but I think we'll survive one night."

He chuckled. "Don't let my bodyguards hear you say that."

"Heaven forefend."

"Just so."

"So, tell me about the project in Dubai," she said as they took turns serving each other.

She put pasta on his plate while he served her vegetables. It was all very smooth and domestic, as if they'd been sharing meals like this for years.

He told her about Dubai, enthralling her with his vision for the complex he and his investors were building. "It sounds amazing."

"That's the hope."

"You're a real visionary, aren't you?"

"You have to see what can be, not what is, if you want to reach the top." He made it sound like no big thing, but in fact, it was.

"You don't limit yourself by what others are doing." And she really, really liked that about him.

"Zephyr and I made a name for ourselves thinking outside the box, pulling together projects no one else would have considered."

"That's how I see music, as too dynamic to fit inside some preconceived set of parameters." Sometimes, that garnered her praise and others, harsh criticism.

"No doubt that is why I enjoy your music so much."

Now that was so worth any number of comments from petty critics. "Thank you."

"I don't imagine your father encouraged you to stray from playing the classics."

"No." He hadn't encouraged the composing, either. He believed it diluted her focus. If only he had understood; after a while, making the music was all that kept her going.

"So, how did you get into New Age composition?"

"I heard a George Winston CD when I was a young teen, I was hooked. His music had a lot in common with the classical composers, but he took it a new direction and I knew that was something I wanted to do." And no matter how many fights it had caused between her and her dad, she had refused to give that creativity up.

"And the rest of us benefitted."

She smiled, warmth suffusing her. "I only wish I had a voice like Enya to add to my piano."

"Your piano doesn't need it."

"You'd better watch yourself. I'm likely to get addicted to compliments like those."

"That is a problem?"

"Only for me," she admitted.

"It is no problem so long as I am around to supply them."

"Right." But how long could she reasonably expect that to be?

CHAPTER ELEVEN

AFTER dinner and another lavish compliment about her talents, this one directed at her cooking accompanied by a promise to return the favor, they migrated to the music room. Neo was the only billionaire tycoon she could imagine making a promise of dinner and meaning he intended to cook, not having it catered.

He ran his hand along the Fazioli's glossy top. "Play for me?" The request really pleased her, showing that he wasn't afraid of invading her personal space like he had invited her into his.

She slid onto the bench, letting her fingers play gently across the keys as she always did when she sat down at a piano. "With pleasure."

He turned to face her, his expression as serious as she'd ever seen it. "Is it?"

He couldn't know how much that question meant to her. "It is. I *want* to play for you."

"Do I have to sit in that chair over there?"

"Not if you don't want to," she said uncertainly. Did he want to stand?

Her unspoken question was answered when he joined her on the piano bench, filling her space in a way nothing had in her life except the music.

"Don't hold any mistakes against me. I find your nearness distracting," she admitted with a smile.

"Then we are even."

"I distract you?"

"Near, or far. Yes, you do." He sounded bemused by that fact.

She didn't reply to what was a pretty shocking revelation to her as well. Instead, she started to play. It was a 1940s big band piece that sounded romantic on the piano. At least she thought so.

He listened in silence with a faint smile on his face for a minute before saying, "I like this, but I don't recognize it."

"It was popular in the forties."

"Are you serious?"

"Yes."

"Maybe I should expand my musical horizons."

"I'm always for opening yourself to new styles of music, or new to you anyway."

"You do know that I wouldn't be aware of any mistakes you might make?"

She grinned up at him as her fingers moved over the keyboard in a well-memorized pattern. "Maybe that's why I played it."

"Maybe it's time I upped the stakes."

Before she could ask what he meant, his strong arm snaked around her waist and his thumb began to play a matching beat to the piano music against her stomach.

Her fingers fumbled on the keyboard like they hadn't done since she was a small child. "That's upping the stakes all right."

"Do you want me to stop?"

"Not at all." She could play her music in her sleep. His nearness wasn't going to get the best of her.

She concentrated on the song and tried to ignore the movements of his hand, but when a gentle kiss landed on her temple, she froze. "I thought you wanted me to play for you."

"So did I, but I have discovered there are other things I want even more."

"What things?"

"This." He tipped her head up and kissed her, his lips molding hers with definite intent.

"Oh," she breathed against his mouth.

That was all she got out before he deepened the kiss. They were upstairs and she was only marginally aware of how they'd gotten there. She had a vague sense that she'd been carried, but she was too busy touching him and reveling in his touches to think much about it.

"I wasn't going to do this," he said when he had her naked beneath him.

"Why not?"

"You need time to recover from last night."

"I feel fine." She had a few twinges of soreness, but not anything near enough to stop her from pursuing pleasure like she'd experienced the night before.

But the pleasure wasn't like it had been the night before, it was bigger. She screamed his name when she climaxed and again moments later when he drew a second orgasm from her oversensitized body as he found his own completion.

Then he held her, helping her to come down from feelings so intense her body shook uncontrollably in the aftermath.

"If you ever get tired of being a big-shot tycoon, you've got another career as a gigolo waiting for you."

He laughed, the sound large in her usually silent bedroom. "I'll stick with unpaid pleasure, thank you."

"I'm glad. I don't think I could afford you."

"You are a nut."

"So I've been told," she said more soberly than she meant to.

"That is not what I meant. I do not think you are crazy."

Not yet anyway, but it always came. Sooner or later. That lack of comprehension when she could not make herself do something "normal" people took for granted. Regardless of what the future might hold, she was grateful for his attitude in the present.

"Thank you."

"My pleasure."

She grinned and shook her head. "Oh, I think that particular commodity is entirely mutual."

"Yes."

"Seriously. If I had known sex was this wonderful, I would have taken up with one of the groupies that showed interest," she joked,only half-kidding.

"It would not have been like this."

"Because none of them were the great Neo Stamos?"

"Because no one has ever given me anything approaching the pleasure I find with you. What we have here, Cassandra, it is very special."

She could think of nothing to say in response to those words that would not reveal the depth of her feeling, so she remained mute, but placed a tender kiss filled with the love she could not give voice onto his shoulder.

He smiled and returned the kiss, on her mouth. "I should not spend the night."

"Why?"

He sighed. "I have to be at the office at six a.m. for a phone call."

"Why so early?"

"Time differences."

"I understand. You could leave early," she suggested tentatively, unsure if she was reading his desire to stay right, or not.

"If you don't mind me possibly waking you when I get up to go?"

"I don't mind." And if her agreement was offered with the speed of light, who could criticize?

"Then I can sleep here. Thank you."

She was just very happy he wanted to stay. She'd only spent one night in his arms, but knew it was fast becoming one of her favorite things. Maybe even a necessity. It was the first time anyone had ever stayed overnight, and rather than make her feel anxious it made her feel excited.

Neo didn't wake her getting out of bed. In fact, she barely woke when he kissed her goodbye and warned her he would be resetting the alarm.

He followed the pattern of the day before, calling her at random intervals to ask this or tell her that. At one point, she teased him, "Why don't you just admit you called to hear my voice?"

"And if I did?"

"I'd be even more melted than I already am."

"Then I had better not admit it."

Did that mean he really did just call to hear her talk? She knew she loved listening to his voice. Adored it, really.

The trip to Napa Valley was incredible. The rental house Miss Parks found for them was nicer than Cass's own house, with a truly decadent master suite complete with two-person Jacuzzi. The sunken living room was a romantic paradise and Neo took full advantage of the option for candlelight and low-heat gas fireplace.

Cass discovered that flying on a personal jet did not trigger any of her agoraphobic fears. She also discovered that lovemaking was as much fun in the living room as the bedroom and up against a wall as on the bed. She seduced Neo in the pool, but decided after nearly drowning that the Jacuzzi might be the better option.

She slept the entire flight home. Neo worked.

Over the following days, Neo showed no signs of getting bored with her, or frustrated by her limitations. He continued to call her randomly throughout the day and came over or cajoled her into coming to his penthouse almost nightly. She loved swimming in the pool, so she didn't mind at all. He requested that she use the suit she had the first time and kept it in his private changing room so no one else could. In the event Zephyr had guests. Neo wasn't seeing anyone else.

So, a couple of weeks later, when he suggested she try hypnotherapy as they lay in bed together after making love, she didn't automatically assume he was like everyone else. Trying to fix her because she was not good enough the way she was.

"Bob suggested that a couple of years ago, but I wasn't willing to consider it because I knew he just wanted me to get well enough to perform publicly."

"I do not care if you ever perform for an audience. If you wanted it, I would do all in my power to help you achieve it, but you don't. However, I know you feel the pain of the limits your fears put on your life."

"I would like to go out to a restaurant with you without breaking into a sweat over it, or hyperventilating if someone recognizes me." She'd done well at the wine-tasting in Napa Valley and they'd eaten out there as well, at a quiet, intimate restaurant where no one but the waitstaff would have considered speaking to her.

She knew she'd been able to enjoy those things because she'd been with Neo. Not only did his presence give her the courage to try new things, but he adroitly ran interference between her and others. And he never took her anywhere overly crowded, or that made her get that sick feeling she might not be able to get out.

He was so careful of her and with her. She felt cherished.

"I, too, would enjoy this." But he said it with his arms wrapped firmly around her and she didn't take that to mean he was getting sick of eating in with her.

"Did you have someone in mind?"

"Of course."

She laughed and traced a shape over his chest, only realizing it was a heart when she finished. He didn't seem to notice. "*Of course*. You never offer a suggestion without a full plan behind it."

"Her name is Lark Corazon and she has had marked success treating agoraphobia and other phobias."

"You've met her?"

He shrugged.

Cass leaned up to look down at him. "You did. You met with her. What was she like?"

"A normal person."

"No crystal balls or colorful silks hanging from the ceiling."

"I think you're confusing a hypnotherapist with a fortune teller."

"Maybe. I'm willing to meet her." But only because it was Neo making the suggestion. She trusted him like she had never trusted anyone.

He gave her that look of approval she'd become fully addicted to. "I knew you would be. We have an appointment with her tomorrow."

"We?"

"You do not think I would make you go alone, do you?"

She snuggled into him. "You're too good to me, Neo."

"What are friends for?"

"I don't know. I've never had one like you."

"Ditto."

"Hypnotism is…I don't know."

"Different?"

"Yes."

"And a little scary," he suggested.

"I'm afraid of enough in my life." She didn't want to be afraid of this, too.

"But the idea of being hypnotized is overwhelming."

"Yes."

"Do you want me to stay through the session?"

"Would you?"

"Yes."

And he did, sitting in the corner, a solid presence that made her feel safe enough to answer all the hypnotherapist's questions honestly and then relax as much as she was capable during the hypnotherapy.

* * *

A month later, Cass and Neo shared a table at the restaurant at the top of the Space Needle. She had always wanted to come, but had not been able to deal with the thought of the crowds, much less being trapped in a restaurant that could only be reached or exited via a very long elevator ride.

Happiness bubbled inside her like delicious French champagne. The real thing.

"Lark says there is so much trauma mixed in with my public performing, it could be months or years before it's completely redirected."

"That is all right. Performing is not something you ever have to do again."

Cass's joy just increased with Neo's words. It was official, she was hopelessly, irrevocably in love with the billionaire Greek tycoon. Her Chinese scholar pen pal agreed, as did several of her online friends. The only one who didn't know and probably wouldn't agree was Neo himself.

She didn't let that thought hamper her current pleasure. "I know, but I love being able to do *this*."

"It is a joy to see you so happy."

She laughed. "You convinced me that you would never have grown tired of our friendship regardless of my limitations. You don't know how special that is."

"What was to grow tired of? We went piano shopping. And to Napa Valley."

"Yes, we did." And he was taking her to Dubai for the grand opening of his complex. His contractor had come through and Neo had told Cass he wanted to wait to go until she could go with him…comfortably.

Was it any wonder hope that he might feel something

for her besides friendship sprang eternal in her heart. Some days, she was even convinced he would welcome her words of love, but she always chickened out at the last minute.

"And now you will accompany me to that charity event," he said.

"Tell me again why you are going to a five-hundred-dollar-a-plate dinner to raise money for pet neutering? You don't even have a dog."

"And I don't plan on getting one, but lots of business gets done at dinners like this."

"Just like the golf course."

"A tedious game, but one in which I am more than proficient."

She shook her head. "Anything for business, hmm?"

"Perhaps that is why your friendship is so special to me. It is for me and me alone. Not the business. Not the next deal."

His words warmed her even as they gave her heart a twinge.

She wanted so much more than friendship with benefits and sometimes she thought he did, too, but then he reiterated his stance on their relationship. And as wonderful as she found his friendship, it hurt to know one day he would fall for another woman and she would be relegated to the fringes of his life.

That night, she decided to expand her lovemaking repertoire and when her mouth first touched his hardness, his body jerked in shock.

"What are you doing?"

"I believe it is referred to as—"

His laughter was choked. "I know what it is, you imp," he interrupted. "I am surprised you have decided to offer this gift to me."

"Why?" She licked along the length of his shaft, thoroughly enjoying the flavor of his skin. "I've been wanting to for a while."

"Why wait?"

"I was afraid of messing it up."

"Trust me, there is no messing up."

"Oh, I'm pretty sure there is. I read up on it and I've got it on good authority that a lack of care with my teeth would be a bad, bad, bad thing."

"There is that." For once, he was the breathless one.

She took the flared head of his erection in her mouth and swirled her tongue around it. He tasted sweet and she liked it.

"You taste good."

She closed her mouth over his throbbing flesh and sucked hard.

He shouted, canting his hips upward.

She'd been prepared for this reaction, her hand wrapped firmly around his big erection. It stopped him from thrusting too far into her mouth, but she loved this proof of how much he enjoyed what she was doing.

He'd used his mouth on her many times sending her into spasms of pleasure that seemed to last forever. She wanted to do the same for him.

She'd read about not letting him climax right away and intensifying the effect, so that was what she did.

She was unprepared for him grabbing her and dragging her up his body even as he flipped them, and then thrust into her. He stopped a moment later and swore. "I forgot the condom."

"I've been on birth control for several weeks."

"You did not tell me."

"It isn't something you discuss over dinner."

"It is something you mention to your partner before he has a heart attack making love to you without protection."

"I did tell you."

He shook his head, but resumed moving, taking them both over the pinnacle more quickly than she would have thought possible.

Afterward, she curled up into his side like she always did and faded into sleep, a proud little smile curling her lips.

Neo sat with Zephyr on the side of the pool after swimming laps with his business partner. They hadn't used the pool at the same time in months.

"How are things between you and Cass?" Zephyr asked. "I noticed you're still taking piano lessons."

"Yes." Though he spent as many lessons in her bed as he did on the piano bench. He'd made it a personal competition to see how often he could sidetrack Teacher.

"Is it serious between you?"

"Serious? We are friends."

"Who sleep together almost every night."

"How do you know this?"

"Please, I'm not blind."

He shrugged and repeated, "She is my friend."

"Friends with benefits?"

"That's what she calls it."

"So, you wouldn't mind if she shared similar benefits with other friends."

"She does not have other friends she sees in person." But now that she was overcoming her agoraphobia, that would change, a voice taunted in his brain.

"You haven't hooked up with anyone else since you met her."

"I grew tired of the one-night stands."

"But you don't want anything more than friends with benefits with Cass?"

"What else is there?"

"Marriage. Babies."

"Have you lost your mind?" he asked his friend. "I do not have time for a wife and children. I barely have time for Cassandra. Besides, things are fine just the way they are."

"Are they?"

"I don't want anything else."

"You're sure about that?"

"Absolutely."

"That's good I guess."

That response shocked Neo. He'd been prepared for Lecture 101 on the benefits of married life and family. Not that Zephyr would ever succumb to the institution. "Why?"

"Because Cass apparently decided to go swimming and I think she overheard pretty much everything we just said. I can't be sure, but the way she rushed out of here looking stricken spoke for itself, I think."

Neo surged to his feet. "Why didn't you say anything?"

"I didn't know she was there until too late, but hey. It wasn't like you said anything she didn't already know, right?"

No, but that didn't matter. "You said she looked stricken."

"*Ohi*, I'm not sure the whole friends-with-benefits thing is still working for her."

"You were meddling," Neo accused.

Zephyr gave him an innocent look he didn't believe for a minute. "I was just talking to you."

"Poking and prodding things best left alone."

"Maybe Cass didn't want them left alone."

"Maybe you should have minded your own damn business."

"Maybe instead of yelling at me, you should go fix this."

"And how am I to do that?"

"Start by getting your head out of your ass and go from there."

Neo barely restrained from punching his best friend right in the face. But damn it, Zee wasn't the one he was angry at. It was himself.

He'd spent so many years eschewing love that when it found its way into his life, he'd done everything but stand on his head to pretend it wasn't there. He'd denied any deeper feelings, denied the resurfaced yearnings he'd hadn't allowed through time since he was too young to know better. Yearning for love. For a family. For what others had and he had never known.

Neither had Cassandra, not really. Her life had been almost as barren as his own and still, he had withheld his emotions from her. Why?

He was ashamed to admit it was because of fear. He, Neo Stamos, billionaire and all-around powerful guy, was terrified of not being worthy of his precious pianist's heart.

Just as he had somehow not been worthy of his parents' love. Only wasn't that the thinking of his bruised child's heart? Didn't he realize as an adult, a rational thinker, that surely it was his parents' deficiency—not his—that accounted for the lack of love in his life.

And didn't he owe Cassandra something more than the residue of a painful childhood he'd left behind him long ago?

Silent tears rushed down Cass's cheeks as she let herself into her house. She was furious with herself for crying, but couldn't stop the emotional onslaught.

She knew Neo didn't want her for anything but sex and friendship, only she hadn't been able to help herself from hoping. She'd gone floating along in this little bubble of fantasy that their circumstances did nothing to pop.

He spent his off time with her. All of it. He called her several times a day just to talk. He was still learning to play the piano, though goodness knew he spent as much lesson time teaching her pleasure as she did teaching him music. They made love and spent the night together almost every day.

But the reality was, for him that was just friendship. Nothing more.

The problem was, she loved him and that love was burning a hole in her heart from staying hidden.

She wanted to get married. She wanted to have his babies and work with Dora to feed him healthy meals, but remind him that food wasn't just fuel. It could be enjoyed.

Cass wanted so much she knew she could never have. As far as she'd come with her issues, she was no match for a billionaire tycoon that could have any woman he wanted. And should have one that could offer unrestrained ability to couple him to business dinners and parties, not be limited to an event or two every couple of weeks.

Even able to go in crowded public places, Cass was still horrifically shy and had a hard time putting herself out there for others to get to know. Neo acted like he didn't mind, but that was because they were just friends. Anything more would be unthinkable.

She shied away from the music room and her bedroom was not where she wanted to be right now, either.

She stood in the hall and looked around her and wondered for the first time what she was doing living in her parents' house. It wasn't as if the memories of them all living here together were so good for her.

And yet she clung to the house as a link to the only people who had loved her, if only a little.

Neo found Cassandra in her small study when he finally reached her house. Red-rimmed eyes testified to the tears she had shed and his heart caught.

But far more alarming was what was on her computer screen. "You are looking to move?"

"Why not? There is nothing holding me here."

Paralyzed by unexpected pain, for a moment Neo could not breathe. "I am here."

She gave him a measuring look. "For how long?"

"What do you mean?"

"You'll eventually tire of our benefits and start dating other women again."

No way in hell, but he wasn't ready to say that. He was still grappling with the feelings he'd forced himself to acknowledge. Like the debilitating fear the thought of losing her caused. "We would still be friends."

"No."

"No?" Sharp pain lanced through him.

"Maybe. I don't know. You've done so much for me. You're the best friend I've ever had. You've been better to me than anyone in my life, including my parents. I wouldn't just ditch your friendship, but I don't know if I could handle watching you with other women." The pain in her voice nearly brought him to his knees.

It was unthinkable. "I would not ask you to."

She just gave him a look.

"Do you want more?" he asked her, marshalling his thoughts and arguments so he did not lose the most important person in his life.

"What difference would it make if I did? You don't. You made that clear enough."

"Maybe I was wrong."

"The things I want need something a lot stronger than maybe."

"What is love?"

Cass stared at Neo in shock. "What do you mean? You know what love is."

"No, in fact, I do not."

"But…"

"I have never been in love and no one has ever loved me."

"Zephyr loves you like a brother."

"I have no desire to marry Zephyr."

"You don't want to marry me, either."

"I was wrong."

"What?"

"I do want to marry you. I want everything, but I did not feel I had the right to ask for it."

She started to cry again and swiped at her cheeks. "Why would you say that?"

"I understand business, but relationships are something else entirely."

"You have been so good to me I don't know how you could question your ability to maintain a relationship."

"Do you think I have been good to you?"

"Yes!"

"Good." He looked relieved. As if there could be any doubt. "That is good."

"Neo, even though we are just friends, you treat me like a princess. You would make an amazing husband and father."

"We are not just friends," he said in a voice like shattered glass.

"We aren't?" Oh, please, please convince her.

"No."

"What are we then?"

"Everything. You are my everything and that is what I wish to be to you."

"You already are." She walked forward and reached up to put both her hands on either side of his handsome face. "How could you not know that? Neo, you are everything I have ever wanted, or ever could want. I love you, with everything that I am."

He pulled her close, tilting his head until their eyes had no choice but to lock gazes. "I love you. I have never said that to another person, but I will never stop saying it to you. I was afraid."

"Afraid of what?"

"Not being worthy of your love."

She didn't ask him how he could think that. His formative years explained it all. "Your parents didn't deserve you, not the other way around."

"Intellectually, I know this."

"I'm going to make sure you realize it deep in your heart as well. I love you, Neo, so much."

"I adore you, *yineka mou*, and I always will."

"Even with the hypnotherapy, I'll probably always be shy. I won't ever be a big society hostess."

"It does not matter. I do not want a big society hostess. I want you. And I want a wife…a woman who will maybe one day help me make a family different than the ones either of us knew growing up."

Oh, yes. "I can't imagine anything better."

"Neither can I."

Then he kissed her, or she kissed him…she really wasn't sure how their lips met, but meet they did and it was the most profound kiss in the history of kisses. It spoke of true love, and deep need and hopes and dreams deferred and almost lost, but found again leading to joy unimaginable.

She was in his lap when their lips finally parted. "What is *yineka mou*?"

"My woman, my wife."

She pressed their foreheads together, her fears laid completely to rest. "Oh, Neo. There really was never any doubt, was there?" He'd been calling her his for a very long time.

"No, my very precious woman, there never was. I just had to face a truth that scared the hell out of me. There was someone in this world more important to me than my business, or anything or anyone else."

"It is the same for me."

"I know and I'm so glad."

"Me, too."

"Athens for our honeymoon?" he asked.

"Definitely. We can start working on some of those *bebes* Dora is so sure we are going to have."

"That is one scary smart woman." Neo's laughter filled Cass's world just like the rest of him.

Neither of them had much experience with love, but they would make up for lack of quantity with the quality of their love. They would never take it for granted as others might.

They were truly everything to each other.

MILLS & BOON

MAY 2010 HARDBACK TITLES

ROMANCE

Virgin on Her Wedding Night	Lynne Graham
Blackwolf's Redemption	Sandra Marton
The Shy Bride	Lucy Monroe
Penniless and Purchased	Julia James
Powerful Boss, Prim Miss Jones	Cathy Williams
Forbidden: The Sheikh's Virgin	Trish Morey
Secretary by Day, Mistress by Night	Maggie Cox
Greek Tycoon, Wayward Wife	Sabrina Philips
The French Aristocrat's Baby	Christina Hollis
Majesty, Mistress...Missing Heir	Caitlin Crews
Beauty and the Reclusive Prince	Raye Morgan
Executive: Expecting Tiny Twins	Barbara Hannay
A Wedding at Leopard Tree Lodge	Liz Fielding
Three Times A Bridesmaid...	Nicola Marsh
The No. 1 Sheriff in Texas	Patricia Thayer
The Cattleman, The Baby and Me	Michelle Douglas
The Surgeon's Miracle	Caroline Anderson
Dr Di Angelo's Baby Bombshell	Janice Lynn

HISTORICAL

The Earl's Runaway Bride	Sarah Mallory
The Wayward Debutante	Sarah Elliott
The Laird's Captive Wife	Joanna Fulford

MEDICAL™

Newborn Needs a Dad	Dianne Drake
His Motherless Little Twins	Dianne Drake
Wedding Bells for the Village Nurse	Abigail Gordon
Her Long-Lost Husband	Josie Metcalfe

0410 Gen Std LP

MAY 2010 LARGE PRINT TITLES

ROMANCE

Ruthless Magnate, Convenient Wife — Lynne Graham
The Prince's Chambermaid — Sharon Kendrick
The Virgin and His Majesty — Robyn Donald
Innocent Secretary...Accidentally Pregnant — Carol Marinelli
The Girl from Honeysuckle Farm — Jessica Steele
One Dance with the Cowboy — Donna Alward
The Daredevil Tycoon — Barbara McMahon
Hired: Sassy Assistant — Nina Harrington

HISTORICAL

Tall, Dark and Disreputable — Deb Marlowe
The Mistress of Hanover Square — Anne Herries
The Accidental Countess — Michelle Willingham

MEDICAL™

Country Midwife, Christmas Bride — Abigail Gordon
Greek Doctor: One Magical Christmas — Meredith Webber
Her Baby Out of the Blue — Alison Roberts
A Doctor, A Nurse: A Christmas Baby — Amy Andrews
Spanish Doctor, Pregnant Midwife — Anne Fraser
Expecting a Christmas Miracle — Laura Iding

0510 Gen Std HB

MILLS & BOON

JUNE 2010 HARDBACK TITLES

ROMANCE

Marriage: To Claim His Twins	Penny Jordan
The Royal Baby Revelation	Sharon Kendrick
Under the Spaniard's Lock and Key	Kim Lawrence
Sweet Surrender with the Millionaire	Helen Brooks
The Virgin's Proposition	Anne McAllister
Scandal: His Majesty's Love-Child	Annie West
Bride in a Gilded Cage	Abby Green
Innocent in the Italian's Possession	Janette Kenny
The Master of Highbridge Manor	Susanne James
The Power of the Legendary Greek	Catherine George
Miracle for the Girl Next Door	Rebecca Winters
Mother of the Bride	Caroline Anderson
What's A Housekeeper To Do?	Jennie Adams
Tipping the Waitress with Diamonds	Nina Harrington
Saving Cinderella!	Myrna Mackenzie
Their Newborn Gift	Nikki Logan
The Midwife and the Millionaire	Fiona McArthur
Knight on the Children's Ward	Carol Marinelli

HISTORICAL

Rake Beyond Redemption	Anne O'Brien
A Thoroughly Compromised Lady	Bronwyn Scott
In the Master's Bed	Blythe Gifford

MEDICAL™

From Single Mum to Lady	Judy Campbell
Children's Doctor, Shy Nurse	Molly Evans
Hawaiian Sunset, Dream Proposal	Joanna Neil
Rescued: Mother and Baby	Anne Fraser

JUNE 2010 LARGE PRINT TITLES

ROMANCE

The Wealthy Greek's Contract Wife	Penny Jordan
The Innocent's Surrender	Sara Craven
Castellano's Mistress of Revenge	Melanie Milburne
The Italian's One-Night Love-Child	Cathy Williams
Cinderella on His Doorstep	Rebecca Winters
Accidentally Expecting!	Lucy Gordon
Lights, Camera…Kiss the Boss	Nikki Logan
Australian Boss: Diamond Ring	Jennie Adams

HISTORICAL

The Rogue's Disgraced Lady	Carole Mortimer
A Marriageable Miss	Dorothy Elbury
Wicked Rake, Defiant Mistress	Ann Lethbridge

MEDICAL™

Snowbound: Miracle Marriage	Sarah Morgan
Christmas Eve: Doorstep Delivery	Sarah Morgan
Hot-Shot Doc, Christmas Bride	Joanna Neil
Christmas at Rivercut Manor	Gill Sanderson
Falling for the Playboy Millionaire	Kate Hardy
The Surgeon's New-Year Wedding Wish	Laura Iding

millsandboon.co.uk Community

Join Us!

The Community is the perfect place to meet and chat to kindred spirits who love books and reading as much as you do, but it's also the place to:

- **Get the inside scoop from authors about their latest books**
- **Learn how to write a romance book with advice from our editors**
- **Help us to continue publishing the best in women's fiction**
- **Share your thoughts on the books we publish**
- **Befriend other users**

Forums: Interact with each other as well as authors, editors and a whole host of other users worldwide.

Blogs: Every registered community member has their own blog to tell the world what they're up to and what's on their mind.

Book Challenge: We're aiming to read 5,000 books and have joined forces with The Reading Agency in our inaugural Book Challenge.

Profile Page: Showcase yourself and keep a record of your recent community activity.

Social Networking: We've added buttons at the end of every post to share via digg, Facebook, Google, Yahoo, Technorati and de.licio.us.

www.millsandboon.co.uk